GIFT OF A FAMILY

BY
SARAH MORGAN

MILLS & BOON®

First published in Great Britain 2005
Large Print edition 2006
Harlequin Mills & Boon Limited,
Eton House, 18-24 Paradise Road,
Richmond, Surrey TW9 1SR

© Sarah Morgan 2005

ISBN 0 263 18871 X

Set in Times Roman 16½ on 18 pt.
17-0606-49188

Printed and bound in Great Britain
by Antony Rowe Ltd, Chippenham, Wiltshire

'We both know it wouldn't work.'

His eyes dropped to her mouth and lingered. 'I think it would work very well—'

'No, it wouldn't! I have a child and you—' She broke off and bit her lip.

'I what?' His gaze lifted to hers. 'I what, Kat?'

She sighed. 'We have different priorities, Josh, and you have to know enough about me by now to know that I would never do anything that might hurt Archie.'

If she put some distance between them and filled her mind with something else, then she could get herself back under control. She knew she could. As long as she didn't look at him. *As long as he put a shirt on.* And maybe he should shave too. There was something wickedly attractive about his roughened jaw.

Thoroughly flustered, she took several steps backwards. 'I'm not looking for a relationship, Josh.' She felt breathless and light-headed under his searching gaze.

'You may not have been looking,' he murmured, 'but I have a feeling you might have just found one.'

Dear Reader

To have loyal and loving family and friends around you is perhaps the greatest gift of all and who makes a better friend than a brother?

Men don't always talk about problems in the way that women do, but that doesn't make the bond any less powerful, and that's certainly the case with Mac and Josh Sullivan. They work side by side as consultants in a busy accident and emergency department in a rugged part of Cornwall with beautiful beaches and wild seas. Their story starts at Christmas.

Mac, who featured in **THE NURSE'S CHRISTMAS WISH**, is the older and the more serious of the two Sullivan brothers, and Christmas is always a difficult time of year for him. His life is a mess and Josh decides it's time to do something about that. So he arranges a present with a difference. Louisa. For one month she'll sort out Mac's life. But when Christmas is over, is he really going to let this amazing girl walk out of his life?

For **Josh**'s story, **GIFT OF A FAMILY**, the weather warms up and we move into summer. A fun-loving playboy, Josh is very different from his brother. He loves his fast car, his boats and his surfboard and, of course, his women—and there are plenty of them! Why would he want to settle down, have children and risk losing all that? But then his new neighbour arrives, along with her six-year-old boy, and Josh is forced to rethink his whole life.

The great thing about being a writer is that you get to interfere with people's lives, and I had a lot of fun seeing Mac finally happy and Josh well and truly tamed by a woman and her child. I hope you enjoy their stories.

Happy reading

Love
Sarah
xxxxx

CHAPTER ONE

'JUST look at that girl.'

Josh Sullivan strolled casually along the beach with his brother, his eyes fixed intently on a female surfer, balanced on her board.

His brother shot him an impatient glance. 'Look where you're going, will you? You're worse than the dog and, believe me, that's saying something.' He whistled to his dog who bounded happily off into the distance, barking with excitement while Mac watched in exasperation. 'I swear that dog needs a psychiatrist.'

'What a babe.' Josh ignored his brother, his eyes fixed on the girl who was standing steadily on her board as she swept down the waves with effortless ease, arms outstretched, her long hair streaming down her back. Even from the shore he could see her lush curves, clearly outlined by the black wetsuit. And he admired her style. She was good with the board. *And she looked amazing.*

'It should be against the law,' he muttered, stumbling over an elaborate construction that had been left in the sand by an enthusiastic group of children.

This time his brother's remonstration was stronger. *'Will you look where you're going? Some poor kid spent hours building that.'* Mac shook his head and then followed his brother's gaze with a concerned frown. 'She shouldn't be surfing on that part of the beach, anyway. The currents are lethal. Hasn't she read any of the notices? She should be further over.'

Josh glanced at his brother and wondered if he knew how much he'd changed since he'd married Louisa. 'She's good. And the surf is fantastic.'

For a moment he was tempted to sprint back to his house, pick up a board and catch a few waves himself, but then he remembered his plans. After a busy week at the hospital he'd promised his stomach a decent lunch and himself an entire afternoon working on the boat.

He looked at the foaming surf and wished there were more hours in the day.

Mac squinted out to sea. 'There are some pretty young kids out there. What the hell are they playing at?'

Josh yawned. 'Having a good time, I should think. Loosen up, will you? You used to do dangerous things, too. Before your wife tamed you, you would have been out in those waves, flirting with death and danger.'

As he himself did. He saw enough in the hospital to know that life was to be lived, every moment of every day.

Mac stopped dead. 'My wife has not *tamed* me.'

A broad smile spread over Josh's face as he slapped his brother on the shoulder. 'She's got you on a lead, bro',' he said, using a sympathetic tone guaranteed to drive his brother mad, 'and it's a short one at that.'

It was one of his favourite weekend occupations. Goading his more serious older brother. Seeing just how far he could push and needle before Mac exploded out of that air of mature responsibility.

Judging from the dangerous glint in his brother's eye, it wasn't going to take long today.

'A lead?' Mac virtually growled the words. 'Louisa never stops me doing anything…'

Not long now.

Josh gave him a pitying look. 'You just don't get it, do you? And that's the skill of women.' He spread lean bronzed hands to emphasise his point. 'They sneak around and tie you up in knots and before you know what's hit you, your life is over.'

'In a minute you're going to know exactly what hit you and it's going to be me! And your life might well be over.' Mac's dark eyes flashed a warning and the muscles in his shoulders bunched. 'Are you suggesting Louisa stops me from doing things?'

'Not openly, oh, no, no, no.' Josh waggled a finger but took a step backwards in readiness. 'Women are *so* much cleverer than that. They make it look as though it was your decision. And it's such a gradual thing you don't even see it happening. One night you're joining your mates in the pub for a few beers and the next your feet walk straight past that same pub on your way home for an early dinner. And there's not a decent beer in sight.' He looked sorrowful. 'Just candles, fancy glass and fancy wine. What sort of a life is that?'

'A pretty good one,' Mac said dryly, stepping to one side as a child sprinted past clutching a bucket and spade, 'and do I really need to point out that you love fancy wine almost as much as you love women?'

'I also love sport and fast cars, and women just don't get either of those things,' Josh muttered sadly, rubbing a hand over his rough jaw and noting that he'd forgotten to shave. 'Take cars. When you're dating, women pretend they love them, although the truth is they're always grabbing at their hair and sneaking a look in the mirror when they think you're not looking just to check the wind hasn't messed them up in some way. Then you marry them and before you know it you're driving some bizarre vehicle that looks like a coach and comes with thousands of doors and child-friendly gadgets designed to bring a guy out in a rash.'

'My car does not look like a coach.'

'It will do soon.' Josh threw him a look and gave a dramatic shudder. 'Look at that enormous bump your wife is carrying around. That baby has got to go somewhere.'

Mac frowned. 'She's not enormous.'

'I never said *she* was enormous,' Josh said mildly. 'I said that her *bump* is enormous. And so it should be. She's eight months pregnant.'

'She's *not* enormous.'

There was a flicker of panic in Mac's eyes and Josh struggled to keep his expression straight. 'You know—' he kept his tone casual '—I read an interesting report in one of the medical journals last week about this mother who unexpectedly produced twins. Something to do with the lie of the babies—they'd missed one on the scan. Imagine the shock of that.'

Mac opened his mouth, caught something in Josh's expression and the next thing he knew, Josh was lying on his back on the sand, with his brother glaring down at him.

'Next time you decide to irritate me, step out of the way first,' he growled. 'And if you say anything similar to Louisa and panic her, I won't be responsible for my actions.'

Helpless with laughter, Josh wondered what it was about fatherhood that turned grown men into gibbering wrecks. Then he saw the anxiety in his brother's face and his laughter faded. He hadn't realised that his brother was quite so tense about the whole thing.

'It was just a joke! I wouldn't tease Lu, you know I wouldn't. I love her. Hell, I set the two of you up. What's the matter with you?'

'I don't know. Impending fatherhood, I suppose.' Mac let out a breath and then reached out a hand and dragged his brother to his feet. 'Believe me, no matter how many times you reassure patients, it's different when it's your own. I'm a wreck, I admit it.' He raked a hand through his hair and gave a helpless shrug. 'I worry about her and I worry about the baby. Try having a baby of your own and you'll find out what I mean.'

'A baby? Me?' Josh brushed the sand from his shoulders, appalled by the mere suggestion. 'Nappies, sleepless nights and goodbye two-seater sports car with the top down? No, thanks. Fatherhood is definitely not for me.'

Mac shot him a curious look. 'You seriously think you're immune, don't you? You think you can carry on dating every woman who takes your fancy and that you're never going to get emotionally involved?'

Josh gave an easy smile. 'Hasn't happened yet,' he said smugly. 'Nor is it likely to. Relationships go in stages. The trick is to recognise each stage as it happens so that you don't get caught.'

'Stages?'

'Yeah, first there's the spark. You see someone, they see you and there's that special chemistry, something that makes you want to take it further.' He removed his shades and winked at his brother. 'So you do—'

'Well, *you* do,' Mac interjected dryly, 'not everyone does.'

'Can I help it if women find me irresistible? So you take it further and then you start seeing each other. Then there's the passion.' He gave a slow smile. 'And obviously that's the best bit.'

Mac rolled his eyes but Josh ignored him.

'Then at some point, usually somewhere between the first time she leaves her toothbrush at your place and the time she starts staring hopefully into prams, there's a slight shift in the relationship. Spotting that shift is the key to remaining a happy bachelor. Miss it and before you know it the highlight of your life is buying baby car seats to fit in your people carrier.'

He gave an exaggerated shudder and Mac stared at him in exasperation. 'You're thirty-two, Josh. Don't you ever want to settle down?'

Josh thought of his home, an abandoned lifeboat station that he'd converted himself, slogging away in what little spare time he had to lovingly convert it into a stunning home. He thought of his plasma-screen TV, his high-performance car and the boat he was restoring. He thought of the punishing hours he spent at the hospital in the accident and emergency department and the fact that he lived life to his own timetable. He didn't want to change a thing. 'My life works well just as it is.'

'And does that make you happy? Being on your own...' For a moment Mac's tone was serious. 'Is that really what you want?'

Josh gave a wicked grin that was totally male. 'I'm not often on my own. And when I am...' he replaced his shades in a smooth movement '...I'm resting.'

Mac laughed and shook his head in exasperation. 'So who's the lucky woman at the moment? I haven't seen anyone around.'

'There's currently a vacancy,' Josh said airily, 'but I'm considering a few applicants. I always enjoy the interview process.'

'When are you going to grow up?'

'When Cornwall runs out of decent-looking women.' Josh glanced at a girl running towards the waves in a minuscule bikini. 'Which judging from today isn't going to be any time soon.'

Mac followed his gaze. 'You are as shallow as the average rock pool, do you know that?'

'Me?' Josh planted a hand in the middle of his chest and looked affronted. 'I'm just terribly misunderstood. I'm a dedicated doctor who needs an antidote to the stress of daily living.

You, on the other hand, have turned so respectable since I sorted out your love life that I'm reluctant to be seen in your company in case you damage my reputation as a heartless playboy.'

'You don't choose who you fall in love with,' Mac said mildly, glancing round for the dog, 'and one of these days it's going to happen to you. And I'm going to be there to rub your nose in it.'

Josh turned his gaze back to the waves, wishing he were out there. The sea glistened and sparkled in the summer sunshine and the waves curled and foamed as they hit the beach.

The female surfer was up on her board again and he sucked in a breath as his eyes slid down the girl in masculine appreciation. 'How the hell does she balance?'

'Same way you do,' Mac said wearily, 'by using her feet and her body.'

'I haven't got that body.' Josh shook his head in wonder. 'She shouldn't be able to balance. According to the theory of relativity, she should be tipping forward.'

'Theory of relativity?'

'Yeah.' Josh flashed him a wicked grin. 'The size of her backside relative to the size of her—'

'OK, I get the message.' Mac whistled for the dog, shaking his head in blatant disapproval. 'With you, it's all about appearance, isn't it? She's probably as thick as a plank.'

Josh narrowed his eyes. 'With a body like that, who cares?'

Mac rolled his eyes. 'I can't understand why some thoroughly modern woman hasn't blacked your eye before now.'

'Because I'm irresistible,' Josh suggested, his eyes darkening as the girl jumped neatly off her board and tucked it under her arm, shaking her wet hair out of her eyes. 'She's coming this way. Any moment now she's going to notice me. Watch and learn, bro'. I think that vacancy of mine is about to be filled.'

He gave a wicked smile and Mac gave a grunt of disgust.

'I'll get ready to resuscitate her when she's knocked flat by the size of your ego. Has it occurred to you that she might not actually be interested in you?'

'Are you kidding?' Josh grinned and flexed his muscles. 'Brain and brawn. What more could a girl possibly want?'

He stood still and watched as the girl turned back into the waves, lay on her board and paddled out to sea again without a glance in his direction.

'Obviously losing your touch,' Mac drawled, glancing at his watch. 'Come on. What you need is some cold water on that libido of yours. Let's go home. You can take a shower and have some lunch with us before you go back to patching up that boat of yours.' He whistled for the dog and Josh's face brightened at the prospect of lunch.

'Has she cooked Indian? I love it when she cooks Indian.'

'I've no idea. Whatever you think of my sad existence, even I'm not reduced to discussing menus with my wife.' Mac fended off the dog as it bounded up to them, soaking wet and tail wagging madly. 'But I doubt it's Indian, on a Sunday. More likely to be a roast of some sort. She's very traditional, my Louisa. Hopeful,

down! Sit. For *goodness sake, sit,* you stupid dog!'

Josh wondered whether there was a woman
in the world who would have the same effect
on him as Louisa had on Mac. Probably not,
he decided. He tried to imagine himself in his
brother's position, about to become a father for
the first time. He couldn't think of anything
more terrifying. He'd thought about children,
of course, but only to dismiss them with a
shudder. He just couldn't work out where
they'd fit into his life. And he wasn't about to
give anything up, that was for sure. His job as
a consultant in the A and E department didn't
leave much time for anything else, but what
little time he had was spent with his boats or
windsurfing. He certainly didn't want to spend
that precious time changing nappies. No, his
life worked perfectly well the way it was. He
could do without the whole family scene, although he had to admit that he enjoyed being
with his brother, and his sister-in-law certainly
knew how to make a cosy home.

'Well, whatever she cooks will be delicious.' He turned and prepared to head off the

beach towards the dunes that ran along the bottom of Mac's garden. A series of shouts stopped him and he turned, staring at a group of surfers in the water with a frown.

'What's the matter with them?'

'*Over here!*'

Josh narrowed his gaze and watched as several people dragged a man out of the water and onto the beach. Even from that distance he could see the blood. 'Oops.' His tone was cool but his blue eyes were sharp and alert. 'Looks as though someone's had a knock on the head.'

Mac cursed under his breath. 'It's supposed to be my holiday,' he muttered as they both broke into a run, Hopeful at their heels. 'But it seems that even on my holiday I have to look at an injured person.'

Josh was ahead of him, his powerful legs eating the distance as they raced across the sand. 'Relax. I'll take this one.' He dropped to his haunches, aware that the girl he'd been watching was already on her knees beside the injured man, her hair trailing down her back.

In one brief glance he saw two things. First, that she was a redhead and, second, that she was stunning.

He flashed her the smile that always guaranteed him female attention whenever he wanted it. 'Don't worry. I'm a doctor.'

'I'm a doctor, too.' She spoke in cool, clear tones designed to wither a man at a hundred paces, not even wasting a glance in his direction. 'And you're in my light.'

Josh ignored the smothered laughter from his brother, too intrigued by the girl to care about the teasing he was going to receive later. The sight of her in a black wetsuit was having an alarming effect on his blood pressure. She had a body straight out of a bad boy's dreams.

But she wasn't paying him the slightest bit of attention. She was saving that for the injured man, and as she looked down Josh found himself staring at her thick, dark eyelashes, fascinated by their length.

She was gorgeous.

'He's bleeding badly from his arm. Must have caught it on a rock when he came off the board. He was caught by the wave and the board gave him a bash on the head. I saw it happen,' she said briskly, her fingers gently exploring the man's head wound before moving to his arm. 'It's an artery. He's cut an artery. Damn.'

As she shifted the man's wetsuit, blood pumped skywards and she swiftly applied pressure and elevated the limb. 'It's a very jagged cut. I need something to use as a pad...' Glancing around, she spotted the man's friends hovering. 'One of you take the laces out of your trainers and give me your T-shirt.'

One of the men took a step backwards, looking decidedly green.

'It's just blood,' the girl said, a hint of impatience in her tone, 'and the sooner one of you gives me a T-shirt, the sooner I can stop it. Come on!'

Josh watched in fascination as one of the men meekly did as she instructed. Quickly and with the minimum of fuss she bound the wound and turned her attention to the man's head.

Josh ran a hand over the back of his neck, for the first time in his life feeling totally redundant in a medical situation. He kept waiting for her to do something wrong so that he could intervene, but she was doing everything right and she didn't even seem to want help doing it.

She leaned closer to the patient, her body a slim curve in the tight wetsuit. 'Hello? Can you hear me?' Her voice was brisk and professional. 'Can you tell me your name?'

The man groaned and screwed up his face. 'My head…'

'I know about your head and I know about your arm.' Her slim fingers were on the man's scalp, feeling for damage. 'But now I need you to tell me your name.'

The man closed his eyes and the girl frowned slightly. Then she leaned closer to him and gave a sniff.

'He's been drinking.' Her nose wrinkled in distaste and she glared at his friends who were still lurking close by, looking as though they'd rather be anywhere else. 'Was he drinking before surfing?'

One of them shifted. 'Maybe, just a bit.'

'A bit?' She gave them a look designed to freeze boiling water. 'One of you get on the phone and call an ambulance. He's going to need to go to hospital. I can't tell what's the bang on the head and what's the alcohol. What's his name?'

'Dave.' One of the lads shrugged. 'He only had a couple of beers.'

'Before surfing? He should have known better. And so should you lot.' The girl shot them a look of contempt and then turned her attention back to the patient. 'Dave, I'm going to put a dressing on your head and then get you to hospital. You're going to need an X-ray and some stitches, and next time either drink or surf but don't do both together. I need another T-shirt to bind his head.'

Finally she looked up at Josh and immediately she stilled. Slanting green eyes locked with his and widened as something powerful and indefinable passed between them.

Josh considered himself an expert on all things female but he'd never seen eyes like those in his life before and he couldn't look away. Neither, it would seem, could she.

Mac cleared his throat. 'Earth calling all doctors…'

The girl blinked and dragged her eyes away from Josh, but a betraying pink touched her cheeks that had nothing to do with the hot August sunshine and everything to do with powerful chemistry.

'Have you got anything which we can use as a dressing for his head?'

Josh was having trouble concentrating. 'I— er…'

'Take your T-shirt off, Josh,' Mac suggested kindly. 'It might cool you down. You look a little hot.'

Josh dragged his gaze away from the girl and glared at his brother. 'Take your own T-shirt off.'

'Louisa bought me this for my birthday. And I'm not the one who's overheating.'

Josh swore softly and dragged his T-shirt over his head, deriving some satisfaction from the fact that the girl stared at his muscular chest for several seconds before grabbing the garment and turning her attention back to the patient.

Josh watched her with masculine speculation. He was experienced enough with women to know when one of them was interested and the girl with the green eyes was definitely interested, despite her pretended indifference.

He'd felt the attraction like a physical force and he knew that she had, too.

She was securing his T-shirt in place when they heard the ambulance siren.

The ambulance drove onto the sand and Mac gave a nod of recognition as the crew hurried towards them.

'His GCS is twelve,' the girl told them, and proceeded to give them a fluent account of the patient's injuries. 'In view of the blood loss from the artery, I want to get a line in and then we need to ship him off as fast as possible. He's going to need surgery on that wrist and possibly a CT scan. He's been drinking. Make sure you tell them that in A and E.'

Josh watched in admiration as she found a vein with apparent ease, strapped the Venflon in place and nodded to the paramedics.

'All right. He's all yours.' She stood up, her damp hair trailing down her back like a blaze of fire.

Anticipating the moment when he could get the girl on her own and swap essential details, Josh paused briefly to chat with one of the paramedics who he knew well, but when he finally glanced up, the girl had vanished.

He frowned and glanced around him but there was no sign of her.

Damn.

Mac gave a grin and slapped him on the shoulder. 'Well, bro', that was a first. A woman who didn't notice you. Think you'll ever get over it?'

'She noticed me.' Josh was still looking around the beach. She had to be somewhere. She couldn't have just vanished that quickly. 'She definitely noticed me.'

Where the hell was she?

'Which is why she hung around to get better acquainted. Face it, brother, she's the one who got away. I saw her face when you used your ''I'm a doctor'' chat-up line. She was *not* impressed. *I'm a doctor, too, and you're in my light.*' Mac was still laughing as he recited her words exactly. 'And she was bloody good with that patient. Knew exactly what she was doing. I wouldn't mind having her in our department. That really would be a first. A woman who doesn't notice you.'

Josh narrowed his eyes, remembering that one, intense moment when their eyes had locked. 'She noticed me.'

'Well, she certainly didn't hang around to further the acquaintance,' Mac drawled. 'And apart from the body, which I have to admit was impressive, she didn't seem like your usual type. For a start, she could string words into a sentence. And she's clearly a doctor, and a good one at that. You never date doctors.'

'Only because I can't stand the conversation over the dinner table.' Josh yawned. 'It's much more interesting to date someone in a different profession.'

But he would have made an exception for the girl with the green eyes.

Mac shot him a wry look as they strolled back along the beach to the dunes that led to his garden. 'I never realised you were so in-

CHAPTER TWO

KAT unzipped the neck of her wetsuit and stood still with her back against the jagged rocks, waiting until she judged it safe to reappear.

Only when the two men had walked a safe distance along the beach did she emerge and retrieve the surfboard that she'd left at the water's edge. By then the ambulance had gone and the crowd had dispersed.

Maybe it was cowardly of her to avoid them, but she knew that if she'd hung around then the handsome, blue-eyed doctor would have entered into a conversation that she didn't want to have. The strength of her reaction to him had shaken her and she sensed that it was mutual. She'd recognised the look in his eyes and knew exactly which direction the conversation would have taken.

And she just didn't want to go there.

Did he think she was some sort of brainless idiot? she wondered bitterly as she tucked the board under her arm and walked in the opposite direction along the beach towards her tiny cottage. 'I'm a doctor,' he'd announced in a tone that had suggested that using those words usually delivered a willing female into his lap.

What had he expected her to do? Gasp and faint?

She gave a snort of derision, carefully dismissing the memory of the strange sensation she'd felt in the pit of her stomach when their eyes had met. As if a pair of broad shoulders and a near-perfect bone structure was going to be enough to interest her. She'd met men like him before and she'd learned to keep them at a distance. They weren't worth the trouble.

And, anyway, she already had one man in her life and that was enough.

At the thought of Archie she looked around her and gave a nod of satisfaction. At the first opportunity she was going to take him down to the beach and show him what she'd discovered today. They were going to have such fun together, living in this place. It was a whole new life, as far removed from their tiny flat in the depths of busy, faceless London as it was possible to be.

All she could see for miles was coastline. Wild cliffs, crazy sea and soft grass all blended together to make Cornwall. And it had the best surfing anywhere in England.

A five-minute walk along the beach in the opposite direction brought her to the little row of fishermen's cottages, which almost touched the sand. Kat stopped dead and stood for a moment, breathing in the fresh sea air, feeling the sun burning through her wetsuit, unable to believe that she had the right to call this wonderful place home.

Hers.

She couldn't contain the smile.

It was like a fairy-tale.

Acting on an impulse that was totally out of character, she'd paid the deposit, taken out a huge mortgage and moved in. And now they lived here. She and Archie.

A new life.

Her gaze shifted slightly to the abandoned lifeboat station that stood proudly at the head of a slipway near the cottages. It had been sympathetically converted into a luxury home, and from her vantage point on the beach Kat could see that the floor-to-ceiling windows of the living area gave the occupant fabulous views over the Cornish coast. On the abandoned slipway that led down to the beach there was a boat, obviously in the process of being restored, and a wetsuit lay over a bench.

Whoever lived there obviously had taste and style and clearly loved the sea, she mused as she dumped her surfboard in the tiny shed in her new garden and walked towards her cottage with a smile on her face.

She had a few hours before Archie was due home and she intended to finish the unpacking, shower and then devour the new textbook on accident and emergency medicine that she'd ordered from a store in London. Not that a few hours' reading would make much difference to her performance in a busy A and E department, she thought ruefully, experiencing a sudden attack of nerves at the thought of starting her new job in the morning.

Would it be very different from London? she wondered, and then gave a shrug. Accidents were accidents wherever they happened and whatever the mechanism. She was a good doctor, she reminded herself firmly. She had nothing to be nervous about. Whatever was thrown at her here, she'd be able to cope.

Her new life was about to begin.

And she was looking forward to it.

'So, how was the weekend? Did you manage without me yesterday?' Josh strolled onto the A and E unit early the next morning and grinned at a staff nurse who was just going off duty after a night shift.

'Just about, but it was a terrible struggle,' Hannah said solemnly, removing her locker key from her pocket and jangling it in the palm of her hand. 'I suppose you were sailing or surfing or something similarly wet and watery? Did you have an exciting day?'

Josh thought of the girl on the beach. 'Not as exciting as it might have been,' he murmured regretfully, glancing at the whiteboard on the wall and scanning the list of patients. 'So—we're pretty full already, I see. Did you do any work at all last night or were you leaving it all for me?'

'Filing my nails took longer than anticipated,' Hannah said brightly, but she lifted a fist and punched Josh on the arm. 'For your information, buster, none of us managed more than a snatched glass of water last night, so if you want to live to catch another wave on that board of yours, don't make that remark to anyone else! Least of all the new doctor, who is waiting in Mac's office. On first meeting she seems really nice, and I don't want you teaching her bad habits.'

'New doctor?' Josh was still frowning at the whiteboard. 'What new doctor?'

'The new SHO. She was bright and early.'

'The new SHO...' Josh raked long fingers through his dark hair and pulled a face. 'I'd forgotten the new doctors were starting today.'

'It's August,' Hannah reminded him cheerfully. 'And actually there are only three of them because most of the old lot are staying on, as you'd remember if you could put your mind to anything other than sailing and surfing.' She gave a careless shrug. 'Can't think why they've chosen to stay on, personally. Given the chance, I'd be out of this place like a shot. Talking of which, how's Louisa?'

'Very pregnant,' Josh drawled, 'and Mac is driving me nuts. He's totally lost his sense of humour.'

'He's certainly worried about her,' Hannah agreed, 'and I miss working with Louisa. She's such a great nurse.'

'She's also a great cook, so at least one of her skills is still in use,' Josh observed, thinking of the delicious lunch his sister-in-law had prepared for him the day before. 'All right, I'll grab the SHO, brief her and then we start the day. I hope she's competent. Have a good sleep.'

Josh strolled down the corridor to his office, suppressing a yawn as he pushed open the door.

A girl stood looking out of the window, but she turned as he entered the room and Josh stopped dead.

Yesterday she'd been wearing a wetsuit and today she was wearing the light blue scrub suit worn by all the A and E staff, but there was no mistaking those incredible green eyes and the fiery hair, twisted on top of her head.

'Well, well…' His voice was soft as he let the door swing shut behind him. 'The girl with the green eyes and the sharp tongue.' *And the perfect body.* 'You ran off yesterday before we could be properly introduced. I'm Josh Sullivan. Pleased to meet you.'

He walked towards her, his hand out-stretched, and after a moment's hesitation she slid her hand into his.

Her fingers were slim and cool. Delicate, like the rest of her, he mused, watching with interest as she quickly removed her hand from his. Did she know that she'd just taken a step backwards?

'I'm Kat O'Brien.' Her voice was steady, professional and more than a little chilly. 'And I didn't run off.' Her eyes flashed slightly at the suggestion, and he smiled.

'Well, you didn't exactly hang around to chat.' He cast her a speculative look.

'O'Brien? A good Irish name. Does it come with a good Irish temper?'

Her eyes held his, accepting the challenge. 'When provoked.'

His smile widened. 'I look forward to seeing that. What about the Kat part? Short for Katy? Kathleen?'

'Katriona.'

He nodded. 'Pretty name. Well, Katriona, welcome to Cornwall and A and E. As you're obviously going to be my new SHO, we're going to have plenty of time to get to know each other better.'

Was it his imagination or did her fingers curl into her palms?

'You're the A and E consultant?'

He nodded. 'One of them. And you're on my team.'

Her eyes slid towards the door as if she was expecting someone else to appear at any moment. 'But I suppose I'll be working mostly with your senior registrar.'

Josh gave a rueful smile. 'You would if I had one, but unfortunately we're a bit down on numbers at the moment, so you're going to be landed with me. I hope you like hard work.'

She licked her lips. 'We're going to be working together?'

'Well, if you want to learn something about working in A and E, that is the general idea,' Josh said gently, wondering why she was so tense. 'Although judging from your performance on the beach, you obviously know quite a bit already. Why don't you tell me a bit about yourself?'

'What do you want to know?'

Suddenly Josh discovered that he wanted to know everything there was to know. He wanted to know whether she was always so tense and what it took to get her to relax. He wanted to know what made her laugh and what made her cry. He wanted to know what made her happy. *He wanted to know what her legs looked like under the scrub suit…*

He pulled himself together with an effort. 'Why don't you start by telling me where you worked last? Obviously this isn't your first A and E job.'

She shook her head. 'No. I did A and E and then a stint in Obstetrics but I missed the buzz of Emergency so I decided to apply for this job.'

'I'm not surprised. Patching up drunks beats delivering babies any day in my book.' He gave a mock shudder. 'So where did you work?'

'London.' She named one of the prestigious teaching hospitals and Josh nodded.

That would explain why she'd known what she'd been doing. 'Obviously good experience. You did well yesterday afternoon.'

She shrugged. 'The guy just had a banged head.'

'He'd also been drinking and, as you well know, drinking and head injuries don't go well together,' Josh said mildly, strolling over to his chair and sitting down. 'I was impressed. So was my brother and, believe me, that takes some doing. He runs this department so you've got yourself off on the right foot.' He watched the faint rise of colour in her cheeks. 'Have a seat. You'll probably find some of our cases a little different from London, but not much. Did you see any gunshot wounds?'

She perched on the edge of the only chair that wasn't covered in papers, as if she was preparing to escape if she had to. 'A couple. They were gang shootings. Just kids, actually.' She frowned at the memory. 'They looked as though they should have been in school.'

'They probably should have been. I've only seen one gunshot wound since I've been here,' Josh told her, 'and that was a farmer who had an accident with his gun. We have quite a few diving-related accidents and, of course, reckless surfers who head-butt the board. Apart from that, it's the usual round of fractures, road traffic accidents, heart attacks—and that's just among the tourists. So what brought you to Cornwall, Dr O'Brien?'

Her face was suddenly shuttered. 'I like surfing.'

Josh was left with a powerful feeling that she'd practised that answer. 'Where are you living?'

'I've rented somewhere.' Her tone didn't encourage further questioning.

Knowing when to probe and when to back off, Josh backed off, making a mental note to watch her interaction with the staff. Working in A and E was a stressful experience at the best of times, but one of the things that lessened the stress was the support that the medical and nursing staff gave each other. Would Kat fit in? Hannah had obviously liked her immediately...

Was it just him she was chilly with?

'Right. Well, let's give you the tour.' He rose to his feet and lifted a couple of files off his desk. 'I need to drop these with the girls on Reception so we might as well start there. Welcome to Cornwall, Kat.'

First days were always so nerve-racking.

Not knowing the people, not knowing your way around or the routine. Not that there was much routine in A and E, Kat acknowledged as she followed Josh through to Reception, trying to keep up with his long stride.

Part of her just wanted to get stuck straight into a challenging trauma case. At least then she'd feel comfortable.

Or maybe she'd never feel comfortable working with a man like Josh.

Why did it have to be him?

She thought she'd done well yesterday. Every time he'd come into her thoughts she'd resolutely pushed the memory away, assuring herself that she was never going to see him again. He'd just been a guy on a beach. Probably on holiday, she'd told herself. And now here he was, virtually her boss. And he was going to be under her nose every day.

She almost groaned aloud at the thought.

He was a man designed for maximum impact. Staggeringly handsome and more than a little disturbing. With that glossy dark hair and that wicked smile, he reminded her of a pirate. She could imagine him standing on the deck of a ship, planning daring escapes, plunder and the seduction of women. And as for those blue eyes—the way he looked at her made her insides feel funny.

Kat closed her eyes, irritated with herself. *What was the matter with her?* She wasn't one to dream about pirates! In fact, she had her feet well and truly on the ground. If a man was good-looking, she just didn't notice, and the reason she didn't notice was because she wasn't interested. She wasn't on the market.

She was happy with Archie and men like Josh Sullivan held no appeal for her.

But judging from the way the receptionist's eyes lit up when she saw the young consultant, she was in a minority of one. Clearly he was everyone else's idea of a heartthrob.

'Hi, Josh.' A girl wearing a badge saying PAULA, SENIOR RECEPTIONIST, A AND E beamed in his direction. 'Glad you're finally here. There's lots going on. That's why I'm hiding away here in the back office, rather than manning Reception. I'm thinking of locking the doors and putting up a ''closed'' sign.'

'Well, we've got an extra pair of hands to help us clear the decks,' Josh said easily, smiling at Kat. 'Say hello to Dr O'Brien. She's just joined us. This is Paula. She runs the place and keeps us all in order. Anything you need to know, start with her. This is her control room. Out there...' He jerked his head and gave a shudder. 'That's the battlefront, staffed by her generals.'

Kat felt some of the tension melt away under Paula's friendly smile. 'Hello, Paula.'

'She's come all the way from grimy London,' Josh said, dumping the files on Paula's desk. 'But I'm sure she'll soon recover. Here you are. Don't say I never give you anything.'

'You finally finished with them? You're a star.' Paula took the files and stacked them neatly. 'Did Mac take a look?'

'The only thing my brother looks at these days is his pregnant wife,' Josh drawled, turning to Kat. 'Mac is a senior consultant here and Louisa, his wife, worked here as a nurse until a few weeks ago.'

'She's on maternity leave?'

'Pottering round the house, waiting for it all to happen. Never seen a woman so big in my life. She's giving birth to a hippo, no doubt about it.' Josh sprawled in a vacant chair and turned his attention back to Paula. 'So how's Geoff?'

Paula's smile faded and she gave a little shrug. 'Not great at the moment, to be honest. He's very down, but I suppose that's natural.

I do my best to be upbeat, but it's pretty hard in the circumstances.'

Josh's eyes narrowed. 'Has he been back to the neurologist?'

'He's got an appointment tomorrow morning.'

'Do you need time off?'

Paula shook her head and looked away, shuffling some papers. 'It's fine. His mum is taking him.'

'Why aren't you taking him?'

Paula hesitated and her hands stilled. 'We're too busy, Josh.' Her voice cracked slightly and she cleared her throat. 'You know what this place is like in the summer—it's the crazy season. Five million tourists all deciding to do stupid things at the same time.'

Josh grinned and stretched long legs out in front of him. 'Slack day, then.'

Paula laughed in response to his humour but her eyes were strained. 'Absolutely.'

'You're to take the morning off,' Josh said quietly, his blue eyes suddenly serious and his voice firm. 'I'll poach from one of the other departments to cover you and I'll clear it with

Mac.' He stood up and put an arm round her shoulder, giving her a quick hug. 'Take the time you need but come and find me afterwards and we can talk about it. It must be the pits for you both.'

Kat saw Paula struggle with tears. 'You can't give me the morning off.'

'Just did.'

'But—'

Josh stifled a yawn. 'You're boring me now, Paula.'

Paula wiped her eyes discreetly and blew her nose. 'Thanks, Josh.'

'No thanks needed. And I hope it isn't as bad as you're anticipating. Right, well, that's enough staff bonding for one morning.' Lightening the atmosphere, Josh winked at Paula and walked towards the door, gesturing for Kat to follow him. 'See you girls later.'

They walked back into the main area which was the hub of the department, Josh moving to one side as a staff nurse scurried past, clutching a pile of brown X-ray folders.

Kat was still thinking about what she'd witnessed. 'Her husband is ill?'

'He has MS.'

Multiple sclerosis. Kat made a sympathetic noise. 'Is he bad?'

'He has the relapsing and remitting variety so he has patches where he's good, but he's relapsed twice this year so he's being assessed for beta interferon.'

Kat nodded. 'It's not an area I know much about.'

Josh gave a rueful smile. 'Frankly, neither did I until Paula's husband was diagnosed a year ago. Then I rapidly became best friends with our local neurologist and picked his brains. He's a good chap. He's helped them a lot.'

Kat hid her surprise. He'd done that for a colleague?

'Anyway...' He smiled in her direction. 'Quick tour and then we'll try and make a dent in the mass of patients in the waiting room. Like most A and E departments, we run a triage system here so the triage nurse assesses everyone when they arrive and decides on the urgency of their case. But I'm a bit of a control freak so I still cast an eye over the stretcher cases when I arrive. Let's start by showing you Resus…'

He shouldered open the swing doors that led to the resuscitation room but before he could speak a nurse hurried up to him.

'Ambulance Control just called. They're bringing in a girl found collapsed on the beach. There was a party last night—plenty of drink—and her friends left her to sleep it off. She's semi-conscious and won't wake up properly.'

Josh dragged on gloves and threw an apologetic look in Kat's direction. 'So much for showing you around.' He turned back to the nurse. 'Get the team together.'

As he finished speaking the doors to Resus crashed open and the ambulance crew hurried in with the girl on a stretcher, followed by a flurry of A and E staff. Swiftly the paramedics transferred her to the trolley.

'This is Holly Bannister, seventeen years of age, on holiday for a few days with her friends. She's been in and out of consciousness, very agitated, GCS of six,' the paramedic handed over, detailing their observations since they'd been called to the girl.

'Any relatives?'

'Just a group of friends in Reception,' the paramedic told them, and Josh gave a grim smile as he checked the girl's airway.

'I have a suspicion that she needs to advertise for new friends. OK, folks, I want an ECG a blood pressure and a temperature. Make that a rectal temperature. Kat...' he lifted his eyes from his assessment of the patient '...I want you to talk to those friends. Find out what happened. I want to know everything there is to know about last night's beach party, but most of all I want to know what she took.'

'What she took?' Kat looked at the teenager, who was now writhing and thrashing on the trolley. 'You think she's taken drugs?'

'Almost certainly. My money's on MDMA—ecstasy. She's agitated, hypertonic, sweating, dilated pupils...' He looked at the nurse who was checking the girl's observations. 'Temperature?'

'Thirty-nine point five.'

Josh nodded. 'Let's get a line in and then calculate her weight and give her 1 milligram dantrolene per kilogram IV.'

Kat slipped out of Resus and went to find the friends. There were two of them, one dark and one blonde, and they were huddled in Reception, looking the worse for wear. Kat looked at Paula. 'Where can I talk to a couple of teenagers?'

'Take them into the relatives' room,' Paula said immediately, handing her a key. 'Back through the door and first on your left. Let me know if you need tea.'

Kat smiled her thanks but she had a feeling that it wasn't tea the teenagers needed, it was a good shake.

She walked over to them. 'Are you with Holly?'

The dark-haired girl gave a sheepish nod. 'Is she OK?'

'Not at the moment,' Kat said coolly. 'I need some information. Do you mind coming with me, please?'

They exchanged wary looks but followed her without argument, each of the girls dressed in the traditional teenage 'uniform' of strappy tops, hipster jeans and big belts, and wearing the obligatory bored expression.

'All right.' Kat closed the door and turned to look at them. 'You don't need me to tell you that Holly's very ill.'

The blonde girl was chewing gum. She glanced at the other and then gave what was supposed to be a casual shrug, but Kat caught the fear in her eyes. 'She just had too much to drink and she isn't used to it.' She transferred her gum to the other side of her mouth. 'It's no big deal.'

Kat kept her tone neutral. 'What was she drinking?'

'I dunno.' The girl shrugged again, her expression sulky. 'Alcopops mostly. It was a pretty wild party. Whatever was going. I wasn't really watching.'

In other words, she'd been drinking herself. For a moment Kat tried to remind herself that these were young kids, just beginning to push at the traces, test the limits. Was she being too hard on them? Then she remembered the girl lying in Resus and the grim look on Josh's face.

They needed to know that pushing at the traces had consequences. 'Who arranged the party?'

The blonde girl rolled her eyes. 'Like we're going to tell *you* that! I *don't* think so!'

Kat kept her voice steady. 'If you want to help Holly, you'll tell me. I'm not the enemy here.'

The girls exchanged looks again and the one chewing gum gave a careless shrug. 'Some guy we met in one of the pubs. He throws parties all the time on the beach.'

'And was he offering drugs as well as alcohol?'

There was a sulky silence but Katy saw the panic in the dark-haired girl's eyes and decided that she was the one with a conscience. 'Holly is really ill,' she said quietly, 'and we need to know everything we can if we're going to make her better. We need your help. Anything you can tell us might help. Anything.'

'If?' The girl stopped chewing and looked at her in alarm. Smudges of the previous night's make-up darkened her eyes and her face was alarmingly pale. She looked tired and very much the worse for wear. 'What do you mean, *if?* She's going to be all right, isn't she?'

Kat shrugged, unable to give the reassurance the girl was looking for. 'I have no idea, but if she's taken drugs and you know anything about it, now is the time to tell me.'

The girl swallowed, her breathing rapid, indecision flickering over her white features. 'She took E,' she blurted out suddenly, 'but it couldn't be that. She's taken it before and she's always been fine.'

Ecstasy.

So Josh had been right in his initial assessment, Kat thought. He was obviously smart as well as good-looking. Or maybe drug-taking on the beach was a common occurrence in this part of Cornwall? She had no idea, and made a mental note to ask him about it at the first opportunity.

The other girl closed her eyes and gave a sigh of exasperation. 'Oh, for *God's* sake, Tina.'

'Well, what was I supposed to do?' Tina turned on her defensively, her make-up smudging as the tears started to fall. 'I'm not going to stand around here while Holly dies, am I? I don't want that on my conscience, thanks very much.' She gave a little sob and wrapped her arms around herself, looking more like a child than a teenager.

'Oh, get a life. She is *so* not going to *die,*' the other girl said in a derisive tone, and Kat shot her a cold look.

'She could do. Have you any idea how dangerous drugs are?'

The girl rolled her eyes defiantly. 'She's just *drunk,* that's all…'

'How many did she take? Do you know?' Realising that she stood more chance with Tina, Kat directed her questioning towards the other girl. 'If you know, please tell me. It's really important.'

Tina stared at the floor. 'One,' she mumbled, not looking at her friend, 'just the one. Then she just keeled over. We all just thought she was drunk. She's taken them before and she was OK.'

Kat let out a long breath but gave Tina a smile. 'Thank you for telling me the truth, that was very brave of you. Why don't you go back out to Reception and get yourselves some water from the machine? It might make you feel better. We'll let you know how she is as soon as there's some news.' She walked towards the door and opened it, pausing in the entrance. 'Oh, one other thing. Do you have the phone number of her parents? We're going to need to call them.'

Tina blanched and the other girl shook her head, her jaw lifted in a stubborn tilt. 'You're joking, right?' Her tone was nothing short of rude and confrontational. '*No way* are you phoning her parents. You can forget it!'

Kat resisted the temptation to shake the girl. 'They need to know that their daughter is in hospital—'

'But we can't! We're not even supposed to be here,' Tina blurted out, panic flitting across her face, her voice choked with tears. 'Our parents think we're having a sleepover with a girl in our class. They don't even know we're in Cornwall.'

Kat sighed and ran a hand over the back of her neck. What a mess. 'I'm sorry,' she said gently, 'but we need to inform her parents. I'm sure if you give it some thought, you'll understand that.'

Tina burst into tears and the other girl sat down on a chair with a plop, her face suddenly white.

'My dad'll kill me,' she muttered, lifting her head and glaring at Tina. 'This is your bloody fault! You never should have given her the stuff. You were *so* out of order!'

'I didn't give it to her,' Tina choked, tears streaming down her face, and Kat took a deep breath, deciding that she had no choice but to intervene.

'Look, it's important that I tell the team that she's taken ecstasy, so I'm going to do that now, and when I come back I want the phone number of her parents, OK?'

One glance at their ashen, sulky faces told her that it clearly wasn't OK at all, but she decided that she didn't have time for them at the moment. Holly was the priority.

'Paula...' She stuck her head into Reception. 'Can someone keep half an eye on those two for a moment, please? I need to go back to Resus and speak to Josh.'

'No problem. I'll do it myself.' Paula stood up and Kat gave her a grateful smile then walked briskly back to Resus.

It was a hive of activity, with Josh delivering instructions in cool, calm tones that kept everyone focused.

'Kat?' He glanced in her direction and raised a dark eyebrow. 'Tell me you've got news for me.'

'Ecstasy,' she said immediately, and he gave a nod, a flicker of respect in his eyes as he looked at her. Clearly he'd anticipated that she'd have trouble extracting the information from the teenagers.

'Anything else?'

'Alcopops. It appears she lost consciousness quite early on in the evening, but they all assumed she was drunk.'

'Presumably they were all too drunk to notice the difference,' Josh said wearily. 'Remind me to have a word with Doug, our community policeman. They need to keep a closer eye on the beach in the evenings. OK, folks, let's give her that sodium bicarb.'

There was a flurry of activity and one of the nurses glanced at the machine with a frown. 'She has severe tachycardia, Josh.'

Kat looked at the machine and noticed that the girl's heart rate was incredibly fast.

'Let's give her 5 milligrams of metoprolol IV,' Josh instructed calmly, his blue gaze flickering first to the machine and then back to the girl on the trolley. 'Her blood pressure is going up, too. Let's try some nifedipine and then we need to get a CT scan before we transfer her to Intensive Care. My guess is she'll show cerebral oedema.'

'Kat?' Paula popped her head round the door at that moment and held out a piece of paper. 'There's the number you were after.'

'You're a genius!' Kat took the paper and smiled at the woman. 'How did you do it?'

Paula gave a modest shrug. 'Appealed to the conscience of the little dark-haired one. She's not such a tough nut as the other one.'

Kat read the number on the paper and gave a sigh. 'I suppose I'd better phone and tell them where their daughter is.'

'Is that the parents?' Josh checked the ECG reading and then glanced across at her. 'If so, you definitely need to call them. They need to get down here. After the CT scan we're transferring her to Intensive Care. She's going to need ventilating. Do you want me to ring the parents or are you OK with that?'

Kat shook her head. 'I can do it.'

Just about the worst job in the A and E department, she reflected, but she could do it.

She called the parents, gave them the barest information but tried not to worry them, and then returned to Resus to find that they were preparing Holly for a CT scan of her brain.

The girl was unconscious now and something about her pale face tugged at Kat's heart.

She turned to Josh. 'Will she be OK, do you think?'

He gave a shrug. 'Who knows?' His voice was hard. 'Drugs aren't to be messed with.'

'Weird really...' Kat frowned. 'This place is so far away from the streets of London and yet you have the same problems as a big city.'

'In some ways we have more problems.' Josh scanned a blood result that someone handed him. 'That looks a bit better. Where were we?' He glanced at her, momentarily distracted from their conversation. 'Oh, yes, the problems of living in a seaside town. Unfortunately, because we have such good surfing beaches, inevitably we attract a pretty lively crowd. A young crowd. Generally it's all pretty harmless but not always, and there are always unscrupulous individuals out to make money from the unwary. The main problem is usually alcohol. Teenagers come down here to surf and party and they over-indulge. Saturday nights are the worst.'

Kat gave a rueful smile. 'I can imagine.'

He looked at her. 'It won't be anything you haven't seen before. Teenagers behave like teenagers. It's just the setting that's different. Are the parents coming?'

'They're on their way,' Kat told him. 'They live about two hours away. They didn't even know Holly was here. The girls said they were having an extended sleepover with a friend at home and then caught the train down here.'

Josh winced. 'Ouch. Well, they always say that your sins will find you out.'

Finally the patient was transferred, but that seemed to be a signal for the whole of Cornwall to have accidents and the rest of the day was frantically busy.

By the end of her shift Kat's feet were aching, her head was throbbing and her stomach was rumbling from lack of food.

And she'd thought London was busy…

Josh let out a long breath and glanced at the clock. 'Long day. I'm conscious that we didn't have a chance to talk at all. Or eat. Why don't we go for a drink? There's a lovely pub a very short drive from here. Sells great food. I can answer all those questions you haven't even had time to ask.'

Kat stiffened, immediately on the defensive. Was he asking her out? 'I don't think so. I don't—' She broke off and he lifted an eyebrow in that slightly mocking, sexy way designed to test the resolve of the strongest female.

'You don't what?' His voice was soft. 'You don't drink? You don't drink with colleagues? Or you don't drink with me? Which is it, Dr O'Brien?'

Her mind went completely blank. She wasn't used to playing games with men and she had a feeling he was playing games. 'I have to get home.'

'And is there someone at home waiting for you, Kat?' His eyes scanned her face and she felt something shift in her stomach. An awareness that she instantly dismissed.

'Archie.' She said the name firmly as if to remind herself as much as him. 'Archie is waiting for me. Thanks for today, Dr Sullivan.'

Even though they hadn't had time for a conversation, she'd learned a great deal just from watching him work. She'd seen enough to know that, whatever else he might be, Josh Sullivan was an excellent doctor. He used instinct as well as experience and training, and those instincts were obviously good.

'Call me Josh.' He smiled, and there was more than a hint of the pirate in that smile. 'We're very informal here, but I'm sure you already know that.'

She did know that, but somehow calling him Josh implied an intimacy that she didn't want.

There was no way she was becoming intimate with Josh Sullivan.

Prickly, Josh thought as he walked towards his office to make a start on the mountain of paperwork that awaited him. If he had to find one word to describe Kat O'Brien, it would be 'prickly'. Like a thorn bush, it was impossible to get too close without risking physical injury.

He sprawled in the chair and narrowed his eyes as he mentally examined the facts.

She was fine from a professional point of view. More than fine. She'd handled those teenagers extremely well and, from what he'd seen so far, her clinical skills were excellent—but the minute they moved from the subject of work the barriers had come up and she'd frozen him out.

Was that because of Archie?

Josh leaned forward and flicked on the computer. The fact that she was obviously involved with someone disappointed him more than he would have anticipated.

She wasn't available, he told himself firmly, pushing away memories of her body in the black wetsuit. All right, so she had legs to die for and curves designed to drive a man out of his mind, but she was already taken, so as far as Josh was concerned that was the end of it. He didn't poach.

Katriona O'Brien was a colleague, nothing more, and that was the way she was going to stay.

CHAPTER THREE

KAT paid the babysitter and then tiptoed up-stairs and peeped round the door of the bed-room.

'You can come in,' a sleepy voice said from the bed. 'I'm not asleep.'

She slid inside and sat on the bed, wincing as she sat on a plastic boat. 'Well you should be asleep, young man!' She moved the boat and added it to the pile of toys in the box by the bed. 'It's really late.'

'I wanted to stay awake until you came home.'

She winced, wrestling with the guilt that went hand in hand with single motherhood and the need to earn a living. 'I got held up at the hospital.'

'Lots of people having accidents.' He nod-ded wisely. 'Did you fix them?'

She smiled at the question. 'I did my best. How was your day at summer camp? Did you meet anyone nice?'

Because it was the summer holidays she'd been forced to find Archie somewhere to go during the week, and fortunately she'd found a wonderful children's 'camp' run by a team of teachers from the local primary school. Given that Archie would be attending the same school from September, it had seemed like an ideal solution.

'I did magic.'

'What sort of magic?' Unable to resist touching him, she smoothed his hair gently, thinking that in the dark like this, snuggled in pyjamas covered in boats, he still seemed like her baby. But she knew he was growing up very fast and she was making the most of every single moment. 'How did you get to be six? Tell me that. Last time I looked you were still a baby.'

'Magic.' Archie looked at her, his eyes huge. 'Did you know that I can make myself invisible whenever I want to?'

'Really?' Kat looked impressed. 'Wow, I bet that's really useful.'

He nodded. 'I did it today in camp. Twice.'

She lifted a hand to free her hair and it tumbled in waves over her shoulders. There was a frown in her eyes as she listened to him. 'Are you having problems making friends, sweetheart?' She'd worried like mad about uprooting him but Archie was such a friendly child she'd assured herself that he'd soon settle in. 'Who did you eat lunch with?'

'A boy called Thomas.' Archie sighed. 'He turned me into a chatterbox.'

Knowing that her son never stopped talking, Kat hid the smile. 'How did he do that?'

'Well, he kept talking to me so I had to talk back instead of listening to the captain.'

Kat smiled. The summer camp was run along the lines of a ship with a 'captain' and 'mates'. They were obviously very creative.

'And did the ''captain'' tell you off?'

Archie shook her head. 'Not once I explained I'm not normally a chatterbox. Anyway...' he stifled a yawn '...camp is different to school. No one tells you off. It's cool.'

Relieved that he was obviously enjoying himself, Kat felt herself relax. At least that was one less thing to worry about. 'And what did you do?'

'They taught us knots. The bunny runs round the tree and goes back down his hole. Or something like that.' Archie wriggled further under the covers. 'I had chicken nuggets for lunch. With curly chips.'

'Delicious.' Kat thought of her own day. Lunch had been nothing more than a hopeful thought and a few chocolates from a box a patient had left for the staff. Her stomach was growling in protest. She tucked the lightweight duvet round her son and stood up. 'You need to get some sleep now. I'll see you in the morning.'

'Can we go to the beach?'

'Not tomorrow because I'm working and you're in camp. But on Saturday…' she smiled and bent to kiss him '…we'll spend the whole day there. And you'll love it.'

'Sandcastles?'

'Absolutely.'

'Big ones?'

'Definitely.'

'And a picnic?'

Kat flicked on the nightlight. 'And a picnic. Now, go to sleep or you'll be far too tired to be any fun.'

'Mum?' His voice stopped her in the doorway.

'What?'

'Can we go sailing? Please? In a real boat? I've learned the knots in camp.'

Kat scanned the room, her eyes taking in the curtains covered in boats, the blue duvet covered in boats and the various plastic boats that littered the bedroom. Ever since he'd been able to express an opinion, Archie's preference had been for boats.

Unable to resist him, she bent to kiss her son one more time. 'Sailing is pretty expensive,' she said softly, 'but we'll see what we can do, I promise.'

What she needed was to save the life of someone with a boat, she thought as she left the room. Maybe a boat trip would suffice.

She'd read somewhere that there were basking sharks off this part of the coast. Maybe they could take a trip and see some sharks.

Resolving to look into it as soon as she had a free moment, she walked downstairs to the tiny kitchen that overlooked the back of the house. She almost laughed out loud with delight. She still couldn't believe that she could actually see the beach from her kitchen! And to think that only a few days ago the only view she'd had been of peeling paintwork and grimy London, a view that could have been described as nothing short of uninspiring.

Despite the fact the sun was about to go down, the beach was still surprisingly crowded. Wondering whether they were locals or tourists, she filled the kettle and reached for a mug. Next to her cottage she could see the converted lifeboat station, but there were no signs of life. She stared at the building with an emotion nothing short of envy. What sort of person owned a house like that? Obviously someone who loved all things nautical and couldn't bear to be far from the sea.

As well as the boat on the slipway, there were several surfboards propped casually against a wall and something that looked like a mast lying nearby. Whoever owned it was obviously very trusting, she reflected, wondering why he or she wasn't worried about theft. Her stomach rumbled again and she reached for a loaf of bread.

Toast.

It was all she seemed to eat these days, she thought regretfully as she dropped two slices into the toaster. Either that or fish fingers, if she happened to be cooking for Archie. Whichever way you looked at it, her food certainly couldn't be described as gourmet.

She made herself tea, buttered the toast and sat down at the little table that she'd bought for the kitchen. A book of accident and emergency medicine lay open from earlier that morning, and she reached for it and flipped through the pages.

She wasn't a complete rookie when it came to A and E but still she'd felt slightly out of her depth that day. When that teenager had come in semi-conscious it wouldn't have occurred to her that drugs might have been in-volved. First day, she reminded herself, taking a bite of toast and flicking to the chapter on poisoning, determined to read more about the effects of MDMA. She wanted to understand why Josh had ordered the tests he'd ordered and made the decisions he'd made.

He was a good doctor. She took another bite of toast and scanned the book, taking in ev-erything, making a mental note of the ques-tions she wanted to ask Josh the next day.

Josh.

She finished her toast and sat back, allowing herself to think of Josh Sullivan for the first time since she'd arrived home.

Over the years she'd trained herself not to notice men. Not to react or respond. It was a part of herself that she'd shut away. But with the best will in the world it was impossible not to notice Josh. He was a man born to be no-ticed by women. And it wasn't just because of the amazing body, she thought, remembering the moment when he'd tugged off his shirt on the beach. She gave a faint sigh that was en-tirely feminine. If it hadn't been for years of training and self-discipline in the area of masculine attraction, she would have swallowed her own tongue. No, it was more than the body. It was the whole man. The wicked blue eyes, the dangerous smile, the curve of his mouth, the casual self-confidence...

And he knew how to talk to women. He had that way of giving his whole attention, a way of making a woman feel as though she was the only person in the room, the only person that mattered.

Kat shook herself mentally and picked up her empty plate. *What was wrong with her?* She was far too experienced and cynical about the male sex to be taken in by a handsome face and a killer smile. They'd been standing in Resus for most of the day, probably in the most sterile atmosphere it was possible to find. And if she thought that was even close to romantic then she had too much time on her hands. She needed to keep busy. It was the one thing she did really well and fortunately Archie was more than willing to help. No mother of an active six-year-old boy could be anything but busy.

Her life was sorted.

It was tidy. It was neat. She was the one in control.

No way was she going to risk spoiling all that for a man.

The next day was just as busy.

Kat dropped Archie with Mary, the woman she'd found to mind him before and after camp, had a brief chat and then drove the short distance to the hospital. She still couldn't believe that life was being so kind to her. She had a job, she had a cottage that was perfect, if on the small side, and she had found a wonderful woman to help care for Archie. Like all working mothers, she found the issue of reliable childcare a problem and the fact that someone like Mary was prepared to help her out had relieved her load considerably. She was a remarkably young grandmother with time on her hands, and once Archie was at school in September, she would be the one to pick him up on the days when Kat was working. All in all, it was an excellent arrangement and a load off Kat's mind.

A and E was already heaving when she walked though the doors.

'Kat, you're needed in Resus,' Josh barked as he strode away down the corridor.

Kat blinked, wondering whether the guy ever went home. Certainly no one could ever accuse him of shirking, she thought as she dumped her bag in her locker and quickly changed into the theatre scrubs that they all wore for work. If she'd thought Cornwall would be a rest after working in a busy London A and E department, she was fast revising her ideas.

Less than a minute later she hurried into Resus and was handed a lead apron.

'Put this on,' Josh ordered. 'We're just X-raying her chest and pelvis.'

Kat did as he instructed then dragged on some gloves and stuck close to Josh.

He turned to her, his blue eyes sharp and alert. 'Are you confident intubating a patient?'

Kat bit her lip. 'I've never done it. Well—only on a mannequin.'

'Mannequins are good but they're no substitute for the real thing.' Josh picked up a laryngoscope. 'Obviously if it's less than straightforward you call the anaesthetist, but it may be that you've called them anyway and they're tied up so you need to be able to do it yourself if the need arises.'

Kat thought back to the day before when she'd seen him intubate a patient. 'You make it look easy.'

A smile flickered across his face. 'I've had lots of practice, unfortunately. And don't forget that sometimes it's easier than at others, of course, and don't forget that it's always easier in the controlled environment of an operating theatre than it is in the mayhem of A and E.'

Kat moved to the head of the bed, totally absorbed and eager to learn. 'Do you always oxygenate by bag and mask before you intubate?'

'Unless spontaneous breathing is adequate.' Josh handed her the laryngoscope. 'Take a deep breath before you start, and if you haven't finished by the time you need to breathe again then remove the ET tube and laryngoscope and ventilate with oxygen for a couple of minutes, using the bag and mask, before you try again.'

Kat nodded, peering down into the patient's larynx and carefully sliding the ET tube between the vocal cords.

'Brilliant job,' Josh said softly. 'You don't need me to tell you that oesophageal intubation can be fatal. The best way to confirm tracheal intubation is to actually see the ET tube pass between the vocal cords, as you just did. Well done.'

Feeling more than a little pleased with herself, Kat held the tube while one of the nurses fastened it securely in place.

'Very slick, Dr O'Brien,' Josh said, and Kat tried not to notice the warmth in his eyes.

Something flickered between them, something she forced herself to ignore.

She was there to work, and that was what she was going to do.

And work she did. In fact, she worked until her feet ached and she was so tired that she fell into bed every night wondering if her legs would actually move when she tried to get up in the morning.

In contrast, Josh displayed boundless masculine energy, working hideous hours and still managing to find time to keep an eye on the staff.

On several occasions she saw him talking quietly to Paula, the receptionist, and guessed he was offering advice and support. It had taken only hours for her to see what a close-knit team they were in A and E, and she was touched that they'd welcomed her as part of that team without question.

Snatching a quick cup of coffee in the staff-room late on Friday, her last afternoon before days off, she contemplated the weekend with a quiet smile.

'You look happy.' Josh strolled into the room and shot her a questioning look. 'Hot date with Archie tonight?'

Immediately her smile faded. Perhaps it had been stupid and cowardly of her to have let him believe that she had a man in her life, but there was something about Josh that made her feel vulnerable, and during the week she'd found herself noticing all sorts of things about him that she would have rather not noticed.

'We'll just grab something to eat at home, I expect,' she muttered vaguely, watching while Josh poured himself a coffee. His forearms were bronzed and dusted with dark hairs, and she suspected he spent a great deal of time outdoors when he wasn't at the hospital.

On the deck of his pirate ship?

She shook herself. *She was doing it again.* Noticing things about him...

'What does he do? Archie?' He asked the question casually, and for a moment she just stared at him stupidly.

'He's—er...' She struggled to find a suitable answer. 'He's studying.' At the local primary school, she thought, biting back a hysterical urge to laugh. Oh, what on earth was the matter with her? Why didn't she just tell the man to mind his own business? Or, better still, tell him the truth! That she had a little boy she adored and no room for any other man in her life.

But she knew why she was avoiding the truth.

Because that first, unguarded moment when they'd met on the beach had unsettled her, and she had the sense to know that her feelings on that occasion were best left undisturbed and unexplored.

And there had been something in his eyes that had taken her breath away.

Maybe she was using Archie as a defence, but what was wrong with that?

'What about you?' She changed the subject quickly. 'Do you have a hot date, Dr Sullivan?'

She couldn't imagine that this man spent a single evening on his own unless that was the way he chose to spend it. She'd seen the way women looked at him, both patients and staff.

'Tonight I have a hot date with my older brother and his wife, who is cooking me my first decent meal in a week,' Josh said easily, sprawling in the nearest chair and stretching long legs out in front of him. 'And the rest of the weekend is my own, providing I don't get called in here.'

'Does that happen often?'

Josh shrugged. 'Often enough. Two weekends off in a row is like winning the lottery, but one of the other consultants owes me a few favours so I'm taking them while the surf is good.' His eyes scanned her face. 'You look tired.'

'I'm fine,' she lied, reluctant to confess just how exhausted she felt in case he thought she couldn't cope with the job. 'I'm still busy unpacking and getting the house sorted.' And running around after a six-year-old boy. Unlike most people's, her day didn't stop when she left the hospital. But Josh had worked longer hours than her and she'd seen enough to know that he carried a huge weight of responsibility. 'What about you, Dr Sullivan? Don't you ever get tired?'

He gave her a lazy smile that made her heart shift. 'I have plenty of stamina.'

Somehow his comment brought colour to her cheeks and she cursed herself. What on earth was the matter with her?

Thoroughly unsettled, she stood up quickly and walked towards the door. 'Thanks for all your help this week, Dr Sullivan.'

'Stop calling me ''Dr Sullivan'',' he said, his tone mild. 'It's Josh.'

She hesitated. 'Josh.' Using his name somehow made everything much more personal and suddenly she needed to get away. 'I'll see you on Monday.'

By then she would have talked some sense into herself.

Kat woke slowly, still deliciously half-asleep, reluctant to move from the bed. She could have stayed there all day but the sun was blazing through the thin muslin curtains and already it was uncomfortably warm.

It must be late.

Driven by a maternal instinct more powerful than her need to snatch more sleep, Kat forced herself to sit up. She scraped her tangled hair out of her eyes with her fingers and checked the clock.

Then she checked it again.

It couldn't possibly be nine o'clock! Archie was always up at seven, and he always woke her up. He must still be asleep, too, worn out after his first week in his new school.

Feeling faintly uneasy, she slid her legs out of bed. 'Archie?' Still in the strappy silk nightdress she wore to bed, she walked out of her bedroom.

There was still no response and she frowned and popped her head round his bedroom door. His pyjamas lay abandoned on the floor and several wooden boats were scattered on the bed.

He must be in the living room, watching television.

She hurried downstairs but there was no sign of him and she forced herself to be rational. What could have happened to him? Nothing, she reasoned firmly as she pushed open the door of the downstairs toilet and put her head round the door of the kitchen. He was just playing hide and seek, or maybe—

She stopped dead.

The back door was wide open.

Rational thought was replaced by overwhelming panic and her heart catapulted into her mouth. Had she left it unlocked all night? Had someone come into the house? Had…?

Various scenarios, all of them alarmingly dark and unpleasant, played across her brain and she jabbed her feet into a pair of trainers which she'd left by the back door and rushed out into the garden, yelling at the top of her voice. '*Archie!*'

There was no response and she felt the panic rise and swamp her. Think. Think. She lifted fingers to her forehead and raced to the bottom of the garden. She tried to be rational—tried to think as he would. He loved the sea and everything about it, but surely he wouldn't have gone onto the beach on his own? If he had then he could have been swept out to sea and drowned— She shook herself and forced herself to be calm. He just wouldn't have done a thing like that! He must have just wandered into the garden. In which case someone must have taken him, someone must have…

She looked around frantically, forcing herself to breathe, searching for a calm that she just couldn't find. She needed to think and she couldn't think if she was panicking.

She felt dizzy, faint and completely nauseous. More horrible scenarios flitted through her brain. Someone had definitely taken him, or maybe he'd drowned or been—

And then she heard his laughter and she froze.

'Archie?' Weak with relief, she leaned over the garden gate and then she saw him. In the garden of the converted lifeboat station, talking to a man who had his back to her. He was dark-haired and powerfully built and was wearing nothing except a pair of cut-off jeans. Together they were examining the hull of the boat. 'Oh, my God, Archie…'

Her fingers sliding and fumbling with the gate, she somehow opened it and sprinted the short distance next door, her hair flying around her shoulders as she ran, her breath coming in snatches.

What was he doing there?

What had possessed him to go next door to a stranger's house?

'Archie.' She pressed a hand to her chest to control her breathing and stop herself shouting. She just wanted to grab him and never let him go. 'Archie, what are you doing? I've been looking everywhere for you.'

The man turned and Kat took a step backwards. It was Josh Sullivan.

'Well, this is a surprise.' His voice was cautious, a faint expression of amusement in his blue eyes as he looked at her. 'Archie told me his mother was still asleep. I didn't know you were the mother.'

Josh?

She stared at him stupidly. It was *Josh* who lived next door to her?

'I— You…' Momentarily distracted, she stared at him for a moment and then turned her attention back to her son. He was wearing an ancient pair of trousers that were too short for him and his T-shirt was back to front and inside out. 'Archie, what do you think you're doing?' Her voice shook. 'I looked everywhere for you. I've been so worried.'

He gave a tiny shrug. 'I woke up and you were still asleep. I wanted to explore.'

To him it was as simple as that.

'You should have waited until I'd woken up.' She dragged her shaking fingers through her long hair. 'You shouldn't just wander off like that. You *scared* me!'

'It's OK, Mum,' Archie said kindly. 'You were obviously tired. I thought you needed a lie-in.' His eyes were huge and anxious and she felt ripped into pieces with the worry of what might have happened to him.

Oblivious to the fact that she was dressed in her nightdress, she dropped to her knees so that she was on the same level as him. She took him by the shoulders and looked him in the eye, needing to explain why she was upset. *Needing him to understand.* 'You left the house on your own and you…' She closed her eyes, unable even to voice the words. 'How many times have I told you not to talk to strangers? How many times, Archie?'

'But he had a boat.'

Kat stared at her little boy, her chest rising and falling as she struggled to control her breathing. 'He had a boat? That's why?' Her voice rose slightly. 'You left the house without telling me *because he had a boat?*'

The thought of all the things that could have happened to him tormented her brain.

'Yeah, I saw it from my bedroom window.' Archie's green eyes, so like her own, lit up and danced with excitement. He was full of life and curiosity. 'And it's a brilliant boat. Look at it Mum! And Josh has been helping me with my knots. I was doing it the wrong way. I was putting—'

'But, Archie.' Interrupting him and trying to moderate her voice, she gave him a little shake. 'It doesn't make any difference if he has a boat. It doesn't make any difference if he has a whole fleet of boats! *He's still a stranger.*' She lifted her head from the boy, her hair rippling like fire down her back as she glared at Josh. 'And as for you—what did you think you were *doing?*' Her voice rose and she saw him frown.

'For heaven's sake, Kat—'

'Don't ''for heaven's sake'' me,' she spat, releasing Archie and standing up straight, her body shaking with a fury driven by pure relief that her son was safe. She still had to tilt her head to look at Josh but at least she didn't feel at such a disadvantage, 'He's *six years old,* for God's sake! Six years old. Don't tell me that it didn't occur to you that somewhere out there he had a worried mother!' Her eyes flashed and her hair swung with every movement of her head as her temper rose. 'And you're just standing here, *teaching him knots!*' She glared first at Josh and then the offending boat, as if her stare alone would be enough to set fire to it. Tormented by all the hideous scenarios that could have taken place, she dragged Archie into her arms and held him so tightly that he squirmed.

'Mum, you're hurting me!'

'Actually, it didn't occur to me,' Josh said, his tone cool and a frown on his handsome face as he watched her. 'I haven't had much experience with children. He turned up here and asked to see the boat. I showed him. Simple as that. Then we got onto the knots.'

'He's six, Josh.' She glared at him over the top of her son's head. 'Six-year-olds don't just *turn up!* Someone, somewhere is supposed to be looking after them. And heaven knows, it isn't always an easy job.' She turned back to Archie as the question settled in her mind. 'How? How did you just turn up here?' She gave him a little shake, trying to understand how this could have happened. Desperate to protect her child. 'How did you get out of the house? You couldn't possibly reach the door by yourself.'

'I stood on a chair.'

She stared at him blankly. 'You climbed on a chair to let yourself out?'

'I saw the boat,' Archie said simply, as if that was sufficient explanation.

A boat had been enough for him to forget everything she'd ever taught him. She gave a shudder and then looked at Josh, who was watching the proceedings in silence, his broad shoulders leaning against the hull of the boat, his arms folded across his muscular chest. He was stripped to the waist, his bronze skin gleaming from the physical effort of working on the boat. Somehow all that relaxed masculinity made her even angrier. 'And you seriously didn't wonder where he came from? A little boy all on his own at this hour of the morning?' With considerable difficulty she averted her eyes from his body, even though the desire to stare was strong.

He was built like an athlete, all sleek muscle and power, and she wished he was wearing something more than a pair of shorts. They didn't cover anywhere near enough.

'Calm down.'

'Calm down? I was worried *sick.*' She broke off, struggling with a ridiculous urge to burst into tears. *What if something had happened to her Archie?* There was a long pulsating silence broken only by the shriek of seagulls and the distant crash of waves as they hit the beach.

Josh watched her for a moment and then let out a breath and dragged a hand through his dark hair. 'I didn't think. To be honest, kids aren't really my thing.' His voice was gruff and he shook his head. 'He came over here, he was interested in the boat, I showed him. It was nothing more complicated than that. It didn't occur to me you'd be worried. I don't know much about being a parent.'

She felt the anger drain out of her.

Of course he didn't. He was the archetypal single guy.

Sexy, single guy.

You could tell at a glance that the only thing Josh Sullivan would know about children was how to avoid having them. She gave a cynical smile. Men were all the same. It wasn't his fault.

It was *her* fault. She was a lousy mother. She should have woken up. She was the one who was supposed to be looking after him and she'd failed dismally.

Suddenly her legs felt weak with reaction. She plopped onto the bench and sucked in a long breath. 'Archie, you have to promise me you won't do anything like this again.'

'I can't come and see the boat again?' His face fell and his bottom lip started to shake. 'But Josh taught me the knot.'

She saw the hero-worship in his sweet little face and felt her stomach drop. He'd been in Josh's company for less than an hour and already he was looking at him as though he were nothing short of a god. Was this her fault? she wondered. Was it because Archie had no male role model?

Why, oh, why did life have to be so complicated?

She'd thought that leaving London would be the best thing for both of them but now she wasn't so sure.

'Sweetheart.' She kept her voice patient, trying to appeal to his sense of reason. 'It was kind of Josh to show you the boat and help you with your knots, but that's it now. We need to go home and have some breakfast.'

'But can we come back after?'

'*No,* we can't!' She was absolutely sure that the last thing Josh needed to enhance his weekend was a lively six-year-old boy. 'I have lots of nice things planned. Now, say thank you to Josh.'

Archie stared at the ground mutinously and Kat nudged him gently. 'Archie…'

'Thank you,' he mumbled, and then lifted his head and looked at her pleadingly. 'But can we come back again if you come too and if I ask nicely and remember to say thank you?' His tone was desperate. 'Please?'

Kat swallowed, embarrassed and flustered. She ached to give her son everything he wanted but it just wasn't possible. 'No, sweetheart,' she said huskily, brushing her hair out of her eyes and trying to keep her voice firm. 'Josh has a life to lead.'

And it didn't include single mothers and small boys.

Josh shifted. 'Well, I—' He broke off, his eyes on the boy, as if he wanted to say something and couldn't quite bring himself to. He shrugged awkwardly. 'Be good.'

Kat gritted her teeth and then gave herself a telling-off. What had she expected? That he'd invite her son to spend the day with him? She must be losing her mind.

Bursting into tears, Archie tugged himself out of his mother's arms and ran the short distance to their cottage without looking back.

Kat breathed out heavily. 'Oh, damn…'

Six-year-olds didn't have much in the way of reason, she reminded herself wearily. And Archie was such a willing, compliant child usually. But his love of boats seemed to override everything. She stood up quickly, her eyes on Archie, watching until he vanished into the kitchen.

Josh stared after him. 'So that's Archie. I have to admit he wasn't quite what I expected.'

She turned to look at him, her mind elsewhere. 'What?'

'Yesterday you said you were with Archie.' His tone was cool as he reminded her of their previous conversation. 'Naturally I assumed that Archie was well over the age of consent. Obviously you're a single parent. Why did you feel the need to lie?'

She froze. *Why did her life have to be so complicated?* 'I didn't lie.'

'You said he was studying,' Josh reminded her dryly. 'What exactly is he studying? Architecture with play dough? Just for the record, I understand the word ''no'', Kat. You don't have to use a child to keep me at a distance.'

She doubted he'd ever heard the word 'no' in his life, at least not from a woman. 'I really don't want to talk about this now.'

'Unless, of course, you didn't feel able to say no to me.' Ignoring her interjection, he carried on, his voice soft. 'In which case maybe you were using Archie to protect you from yourself. Is that what you were doing, Kat? Didn't you trust yourself to say no to me? You felt the need to invent a romantic attachment?'

She inhaled sharply. 'You have a monumental ego, Dr Sullivan,' she said coldly, and he gave a half-smile so sexy that it made her heart tumble.

'Have I?' His eyes clashed with hers and she felt her knees weaken as a powerful awareness thumped between them.

She stepped backwards. 'I've got to go. I need to talk to him. He's upset and he needs to know that he can't just wander off like that.'

'Ah, yes…' His gaze shifted to her cottage. 'Don't you think you're overreacting just a little bit?'

'No, I do not!' Goaded, she whirled round to face him, her eyes flashing. 'And you're not blameless in all this. He was perfectly happy until you showed him your boat!'

One dark eyebrow lifted. 'So is this all my fault?'

'No. Yes!' She bit her lip, knowing that it wasn't really his fault. 'Well, partly. Have you any idea what it's like to wake up and find that your child isn't in the house?'

'Obviously not.' His tone was level. 'But once you'd discovered he was safe, surely that should have been it. Problem sorted. But you continued to freak out.'

'I did not freak out.'

'You freaked out. You're still freaking out. You're completely overreacting.'

'Overreacting? You think I'm overreacting?' Her mouth fell open and she gaped at him, outrage rendering her silent for a few pulsating seconds. Then she exploded. 'There is no point in having this conversation with you. You obviously know *nothing* about parental responsibility!'

'Fortunately not.' His tone was cool. 'But the boy was just exploring. No harm was done. Why don't you just drop it?'

'Because he's *six years old.*'

He gave a shrug. 'You can't protect a child from life.'

She gave a short laugh and her eyes flashed. 'That's the job of a parent, Josh, to protect a child from life,' she said, tossing her head back so that her hair shone like flame in the bright sunlight. 'And that's what I'm going to do.'

Josh watched her, his eyes on the bright swing of her hair and the swift, graceful movement of her slim legs as she sprinted the short distance back to her own cottage. At no point during the conversation had she appeared to realise that she was still dressed in her night-dress and he hadn't felt it tactful to point it out. Clearly she'd been so traumatised by her son's disappearing act that she hadn't stopped to think about anything but finding him.

For some reason that he couldn't immediately identify, Josh found that extremely touching.

You didn't need to be a genius to see that she was devoted to her child.

It explained a lot of things. Like the fact she didn't hang around after work. Unlike the other young doctors, she showed no inclination to end the day relaxing over a drink. He frowned slightly and leaned broad shoulders against the boat as he watched her all the way to her back door. She was beautiful, gutsy and intelligent, but as he watched her disappear into the house he saw only one thing.

Single mother.

And he had a golden rule. No single mothers.

They wanted something he wasn't in a position to offer. Security. Compromise. All the things that made him shudder. All the things he was no good at.

Josh folded his arms across his chest, remembering the eager expression in Archie's green eyes as he'd shown him the boat, his eyes exactly like his mother's. And he remembered the bitter disappointment in those same eyes when Kat had told him that he had to go home. For a brief moment Josh had been tempted to invite them to spend the day with him, but he'd caught himself in time, astonished by the impulse. He couldn't ever remember wanting to spend the day with a child before.

Remembering the strength of that impulse, Josh frowned, wondering what had come over him.

He usually avoided children like the plague! He was even nervous about the impending arrival of Mac and Louisa's baby because he wasn't sure he could be a decent uncle. He didn't have any of the right qualifications. He didn't like nappies and he certainly wasn't prepared to put his life on hold while they grew up and developed a modicum of independence.

No, children definitely weren't for him.

And no matter how powerful the chemistry between them, from now on Kat O'Brien was definitely off limits.

He was going to stop noticing her curves and her eye-catching hair, he was going to stop noticing the way her cheeks dimpled when she smiled and the way her eyes flashed when she was angry. In fact, he was going to stop noticing everything and he was definitely going to forget that he'd seen her in her nightdress.

He was going to find himself a woman to take his mind off Kat O'Brien, and he was going to do it fast.

CHAPTER FOUR

HE'D seen her in her nightdress!

Scarlet with mortification, Kat gave a groan and stepped into the shower. How could she have done that?! How could she have been so completely oblivious to the fact that she had been wearing cream silk that was virtually transparent?

But she knew the answer to that, of course. She'd only had one thing on her mind and that had been her son. She hadn't been thinking about herself and she hadn't been thinking about Josh.

Perhaps he hadn't noticed, she thought weakly as she towelled herself dry and padded back through to her bedroom. Perhaps he'd been so absorbed in the conversation...

She gave a groan of humiliation and sank onto the edge of the bed with her hands over her face.

Despite the fact that it dropped all the way to the floor, the nightdress was incredibly revealing. She'd even hesitated before buying it but it was so pretty and such a bargain that not buying it had seemed a crime. And at the time she'd assured herself that the fact that it displayed rather too much of her generous curves really didn't matter. Who was going to see her wearing it?

Well, now Josh Sullivan had seen her wearing it.

She gave a sigh and wondered how her new life had suddenly become so complicated so quickly.

Then she looked up and saw Archie standing in the doorway, a wary expression on his face. 'Are we going to the beach?'

Relieved that the sulk seemed to have passed, Kat gave a nod. 'Definitely. Just give me a moment to dress and then we'll make a picnic together.'

Josh probably hadn't even noticed, she told herself as she rummaged in her wardrobe for a pair of shorts and a T-shirt.

A man like him would have said something if he'd noticed.

He would have teased her or given her one of his looks.

No—she dragged on the shorts and slipped her feet into a pair of pretty flip-flops—he definitely hadn't noticed.

They spent the whole weekend on the beach, digging in the sand and playing ball, and Kat took Archie into the sea on the surfboard she'd bought for him.

He was a natural. His balance was good and he had absolutely no fear of the water.

'Again!' Every time he fell off the board he scrambled up again, his face shiny with seawater, his eyes bright with laughter.

They plunged back into the waves repeatedly until Kat judged that they'd done enough for one day.

'You must be tired. Time for lunch.' She ignored his whine of protest and picked up his board, strolling back towards their picnic rug, which she'd placed in the shade by some rocks.

They were tucking into sausages when Archie returned to the subject of the boat. 'Next weekend can I see the boat again?' Ketchup dripped from his chin and his fingers. '*Ple-ease,* Mum?'

She leaned across and wiped his mouth before the red blob could land on his T-shirt. 'No, sweetheart, we can't. But I'll make some calls and find out if I can take you sailing.'

He took another bite of sausage, clearly in gourmet heaven. 'You could ask Josh. I bet he knows a place. He knows everything about boats.'

She didn't want to think about Josh. Didn't want to remember what he'd looked like without a shirt on, his chest gleaming from good, honest physical toil.

Didn't want to remember that she'd stood in front of him in her nightdress.

Her body heated at the memory and she bit back another groan of humiliation. 'Archie, I really think—' She broke off as a large, clumsy dog bounded towards them. Instinctively she tried to grab the remaining sausages but the dog was too quick, homing in on the food with abandoned joy.

'Hopeful!' A female voice yelled from further along the beach. *'Hopeful! Come here! Heel.'*

Kat tipped her head on one side and studied the dog, who was now slavering over the remains of the sausages. 'Are you Hopeful?'

Crazy with excitement, the dog wagged its tail and walked all over their rug with sandy paws, barking madly.

Archie shrank against Kat, his eyes huge. 'That dog ate our lunch.'

Kat nodded. 'Looks as though he did, but he seems friendly.' Cautiously she stretched out a hand and Hopeful slobbered over that, too. 'He's not going to hurt you, Arch, he just fancied your lunch.'

'I fancied it, too.' Archie looked at the empty plates and giggled. 'He's eaten *everything.'*

'Oh, I'm so sorry.' A very pregnant young woman walked up to them and snapped her fingers at the dog. 'Hopeful, when I call you, you're *supposed* to come!' Her voice was stern but the dog continued to wag his tail happily, completely unrepentant. 'Please, could you look a little sorry? Have some sensitivity! Think of the amount I forked out on dog-training classes!'

Kat smothered a grin as the dog trampled over the plates, his paws in the remains of the ketchup. She watched in a mixture of despair and amusement. She was going to be spending her afternoon washing the rug. 'He's been to dog-training classes?'

'Hard to believe, isn't it?' The girl looked gloomily at the dog, who was now nudging her leg. 'He wasn't the best student. Mac, my husband, thinks what he really needs is a psychiatrist. It isn't really poor Hopeful's fault. He had a terrible upbringing and he's very damaged psychologically.' Her eyes scanned the rug. 'I'm *really* sorry about your picnic. Hard to tell from the empty plates, but I'm guessing it was probably sausages.'

Archie stared at her with admiration. 'Wow. How did you know that? Do you do magic?'

'No, but sausages are Hopeful's favourite and those plates of yours are so clean that it just had to be sausages.' She winced and rubbed a hand over her stomach and Kat frowned. The young woman was extremely pregnant.

'Are you all right?'

The girl pulled a face, her hand still on her stomach. 'Not sure, to be honest. I suppose so. Never been pregnant before and I feel like a whale, but maybe that's normal. And the weather is just so hot at the moment. I don't stray far from home these days, but I was dropping something off at my brother-in-law's house and Hopeful bounded off before I could stop him.'

Kat frowned. 'Are you talking about Josh? Are you Louisa?'

The girl looked startled. 'Am I suddenly famous?'

Kat smiled. 'I work in A and E so I've heard your praises sung a few times, and obviously I've heard about Mac. Josh mentioned that his sister-in-law is pregnant so I put two and two together.'

Louisa's face brightened. 'You know Josh? Well, of course you know Josh.' Her eyes narrowed as she studied Kat. 'You're incredibly pretty, so it goes without saying that you know Josh.'

Kat flushed and cast a look in Archie's direction, but he was playing with Hopeful, totally enchanted by the dog.

'I'm one of the new SHOs.'

'Oh. You lucky thing. I miss it so much.' Louisa pulled a face and stroked her stomach. 'I think I'd better be getting back. Walking in the sun with this bump, which, by the way, Josh tactfully informs me is definitely a hippo, is not my idea of fun. Too much sand and Hopeful would make a very unreliable midwife.'

Kat laughed. 'Our house is just up there.' She waved a hand towards the cottage. 'You're very welcome to a cup of tea and then we could give you a lift home.'

Louisa glanced up at the house, measuring the distance. 'Really? The white cottage? You live next door to Josh.'

Archie stopped playing with the dog. 'He has a boat and he helped me with my knots, but Mummy won't let me go over there again.'

'You've been over there?' Louisa stared at him, a thoughtful expression in her eyes. 'When?'

'Yesterday morning but Mummy shouted—'

'Only because you didn't tell me where you were going,' Kat interjected quickly. Not keen to dwell on the subject of Josh, she changed the subject neatly. 'Come and have a cup of tea, Louisa. You look as though you need one.'

'I always need tea. That would be really great.' Louisa tried to grab Hopeful by the collar, but she wasn't fast enough and he bounded back to a delighted Archie. 'I'm just too fat to catch him these days. Maybe we'd better leave Hopeful outside.'

Kat glanced across to Hopeful, who was now being hugged tightly by her little boy. 'Wouldn't it be safer to have him inside where we can see him?'

'You'd think so, wouldn't you?' Louisa chewed her lip. 'Trouble is, he misbehaves even when people are watching so it doesn't always make a lot of difference. It might be a decision you regret for a long time. Are you sure about this? Do you have valuables?'

'He's being hugged by my valuables.' Kat looked at the expression on her son's face and smiled. It was great to see him so relaxed and happy. She gathered up their things and stuffed them into the rucksack she'd used to transport everything to the beach. 'Come on, Archie, we're going back to the cottage. You'd better be in charge of Hopeful.'

Archie stroked the dog's head. 'He's coming, too? Cool.' A satisfied smile spread over his face. 'He's lovely.'

Louisa sighed. 'You're probably the only person who thinks so at the moment. Yesterday he ate his way through Mac's best pair of shoes and the latest copy of *The Lancet*. Then he proceeded to sick all of it up on our new bedroom carpet.' She picked her way across the sand, one eye on Hopeful. 'Mac is Josh's older brother, but I suppose you know that by now. He works in A and E too but he's been on holiday for a week so I suppose you haven't met him yet.'

'Not yet. I've been working with Josh.'

'He's an amazing doctor,' Louisa said, pausing to get her breath back as they climbed the gentle path that led to the cottage. 'And drop-dead gorgeous. It's a lethal combination, as I'm sure you've discovered. Brain and looks. When are you having dinner with him?'

Kat stopped dead beside her. 'Pardon?'

Louisa's eyes twinkled. 'I asked when you were having dinner with him.'

'I'm not!' Kat shook her head, suddenly flustered, relieved that Archie was some way ahead with the dog. 'Why would I?'

'Because you're beautiful and our Josh never lets a beautiful woman slip through his fingers?'

Kat looked at Archie. 'But I'm not available.'

'You're married?' Louisa gave an embarrassed groan and clamped a hand over her mouth. 'Tactless me. I'm so sorry, it's just that you don't wear a ring so I assumed—'

'I'm not married,' Kat said gruffly, 'but I'm not available.'

'You're seeing someone?'

Kat shook her head and Louisa frowned.

'So why aren't you available?'

'Because I have Archie.'

Louisa stared at the boy. 'I see.'

Kat could tell that she couldn't see at all, but she didn't intend to expand on her answer. She wasn't used to explaining her life to anyone. She'd been forced to make her own decisions for so long she couldn't remember what it was like to seek the advice of another person.

'Come on.' She unlocked the door of the cottage. 'Let's have that tea.'

'I gather you met Louisa.' Josh thrust an X-ray into the light-box and squinted at the films. 'Well?'

'I can't see a fracture.'

He turned towards her with that lazy, sexy grin that did stupid things to her heart rate. 'I was asking you about my sister-in-law.'

'Oh…' Kat blushed. 'She's lovely. Really friendly. Archie loved the dog.'

'He's the only one who does,' Josh drawled. 'That dog is one of Louisa's rescues.'

'One of her rescues?'

'She's always rescuing people.' Josh swivelled his gaze back to the X-ray. 'She rescued my brother. Last Christmas. Took over his life. Good thing, too. Thanks to Louisa, we get to eat decent food once in a while and my brother has rediscovered the meaning of life. You know, if Archie is interested in boats, you ought to take him sailing. You're living in the right place. I was on a boat from the age of two. So was Mac.'

She stiffened, thrown by the sudden change of subject. 'I'll bear that in mind.'

She had every intention of making some en-quiries but she had no confidence that she'd be able to afford anything other than a pleasure trip. Not that she had any intention of revealing her financial details to Josh. She organised her own life and had done for years.

He was standing so close to her that she felt the brush of his arm against hers, felt the power of his body.

And what a body.

Heat spread through her and she wished she hadn't seen him without his shirt. She closed her eyes briefly, trying to erase the image. She needed to work harder, she decided. Needed to drive out those thoughts before they blossomed and grew into something she couldn't control. She didn't have room for those feelings in her life.

'Are you OK?'

Her eyes flew open and clashed with his. 'Fine. I'm fine.'

'Your eyes were closed.'

'I'm fine.'

Blue eyes laughed into hers. 'It's hard to check an X-ray with your eyes closed, Doctor.'

She knew he was teasing her but she couldn't respond. Suddenly her whole body was tingling and trembling and she just wanted him to grab her and kiss her until she couldn't breathe. Or maybe she wanted to be the one to do the grabbing.

The thought startled and horrified her by equal degrees and she took a step away from him and locked her hands behind her back just to be on the safe side.

When had she last wanted to grab a man?

Never. The answer was never and the fact that she'd wanted to grab Josh...

Oh!

The fact that she was having those thoughts was too humiliating for words. What if he knew? What if he could sense it?

He was still watching her and the look in his eyes had gone from gently teasing to something infinitely more dangerous and unsettling.

He gave a short laugh. 'Well, well...' His voice was soft and his eyes dropped to her mouth and lingered there. 'This is becoming interesting, wouldn't you say, Dr O'Brien?'

Shocked by the power of her reaction to him, she rammed her wayward thoughts back where they belonged and called on the will-power that had been her fuel for as long as she could remember. 'X-rays are always interesting, Dr Sullivan,' she said, her tone cool, her eyes fixed on the film in front of them. 'And this one is looking fine.'

He shifted closer. Her body sensed his and melted, but she kept her eyes forward. His breath warmed her neck. 'There's nothing there you want to explore further?'

Was he talking about the X-ray or their relationship? She concentrated on the film, tried to ignore the fact that he was standing so close they were almost touching. 'Nothing at all.'

'Are you sure about that?'

It wasn't right that a man should have such a sexy voice. 'Absolutely sure.'

'Speaking personally, I don't think it's going to be that easy.' Something in his wry tone made her turn and she saw a flicker of uncertainty in his eyes, which she hadn't expected to see there.

So he wasn't thrilled about the attraction either.

She gave a cynical smile. Why should that surprise her? Of course he wasn't thrilled. It didn't take a genius to calculate that she wasn't his type of woman. Josh Sullivan was an attractive, single male with a carefree bachelor lifestyle. Why would he want to find himself attracted to a single mother who came with baggage?

'In my experience, life is rarely easy, Dr Sullivan,' she said crisply, 'but as human beings we're given the ability to make sensible choices. That's what distinguishes us from animals.'

There was a hitch in his breathing and his eyes were fixed on her mouth again, as if he wasn't able to look away. 'You think so?'

The core of her body heated and stirred and she struggled to force thinking to dominate feeling. It was a hell of a battle.

'Absolutely.'

His eyes lifted to hers. 'So you're not having trouble concentrating, then? Your body isn't burning up and your mind isn't woolly?'

She hid her alarm. *Was he feeling that way, too?* 'Not at all.' Despite her best efforts, her voice was little more than a croak and he gave a slow nod.

'Well, if that's truly the case,' he said softly, turning his gaze back to the X-ray, 'I'm interested to know why you just missed a fracture the size of the Grand Canyon. Care to explain that, Dr O'Brien?'

Josh manipulated the child's shoulder carefully. 'Does this hurt?' *He'd almost kissed her.* 'What about this?' *She was a single mother and he'd almost kissed her. In public, with the entire department watching.*

Worse than that, he'd almost offered to take the pair of them sailing. He frowned. Had he gone mad? Since when was taking a child sailing his idea of a good day out?

He gave himself a mental shake.

He needed to pull himself together.

Kat O'Brien wasn't the woman for him. All right, so she had curves that should be made illegal and a personality that drew him like a magnet, but she wouldn't be the sort of woman happy to indulge in a light-hearted relationship. She wasn't the woman for him and he most certainly wasn't the man for her. *No matter how good she looked in her nightdress.*

She'd expect him to bond with her son. And he wasn't equipped to be anyone's father figure. The weekend had proved that. It hadn't even occurred to him that it was strange for a six-year-old to be wandering around without a parent. He'd been too busy thinking about his boat.

Josh ran a hand over his face and forced himself to concentrate on what he was doing. 'I'm going to send him for an X-ray,' he told the mother, 'just to be on the safe side.'

He was pretty sure it was fractured.

'An X-ray? But we're on holiday.' The mother looked annoyed. 'Will it take long?'

Josh looked at her, struggling to hide his disapproval. He didn't know much about parenting but he was pretty sure that Kat wouldn't have reacted that way. She would have been worried about her son. She would have put him first no matter what. And she wouldn't have been thinking about her holiday if her little boy was injured.

He didn't think he'd ever forget the expression on her face when she'd come flying into his garden to claim her child. He'd seen terror, relief and a love so powerful that it had pulsed like a force field, protecting her child from danger.

Josh shook himself.

There he was, doing it again! Thinking about Kat and her son. It was time to get a grip.

He pulled himself together and rose to his feet. 'I realise that you're on holiday, but it will take as long as it takes,' he said easily, delivering a smile that melted the woman's annoyance like butter in a microwave. 'But you'll have a better time once he's sorted out.' He handed her a form. 'Follow the green line on the floor—it leads you to X-Ray.'

He watched them go and then turned round to find his sister-in-law watching him, laughter in her eyes. 'Hello, handsome. How do you do it?' Louisa walked forward, stood on tiptoe and kissed him on the cheek. 'She was all ready to moan.'

'You know me.' He gave her a hug, careful of her bump. 'Can't bear moaning women. Talking of which, how's the hippo doing?' He winked at her. 'And what are you doing here? I thought we'd got rid of you once.'

'I'm fat and uncomfortable,' Louisa said happily, 'and I'm here because I need you to do me a favour.'

Josh groaned but his eyes were twinkling. 'The answer is no.'

'You never say no to me,' Louisa said placidly, rubbing a hand over her stomach in an automatic gesture, 'and I need you to take a look at Vera. I would have asked Mac but he's windsurfing.'

'Is he now?' Josh felt a rush of jealousy. 'Lucky devil.'

'He's enjoying his last few weeks for freedom,' Louisa reminded him. 'You'll still be out there windsurfing when he's walking around soothing a baby with colic.'

'True.' Josh looped his stethoscope round his neck. 'So what's the matter with Vera?'

Vera was the elderly lady who lived near his brother and Josh knew that Louisa kept a close eye on her and her equally elderly sister.

Louisa's smile faded. 'I don't know. I popped round to take her one of my chocolate cakes this afternoon and she was very confused. Not herself at all.' She hesitated, chewing her lip. 'I'm worried she might have had a stroke or something. Do you think that's possible?'

'I don't know until I see her,' Josh pointed out gently, thinking how sweet Louisa was and how well she suited his brother. 'Where is she now?'

'Sitting in my car. I'm parked in the ambulance bay.'

Josh rolled his eyes. 'It's a good job you're pregnant or you would have been shot.' He took her arm. 'Come on, then, let's get her out and see what's going on. And, for goodness' sake, move your car before the paramedics start moaning at me.'

'Thanks, Josh. You must be thinking I'm a nuisance.'

'Actually, I'm thinking that my previously uptight, stiff-necked, stubborn big brother is a lucky guy.' He adjusted his stride so that she could keep up, eyeing her abdomen with a curiosity that wasn't all professional. 'Does that hurt?'

She laughed and shook her head. 'Not hurt, exactly. But it's uncomfortable and I've stopped getting any sleep at night because it wakes up and kicks me.'

Josh gave a shudder. 'Sounds awful.'

'It's fantastic,' she said simply, her eyes shining as she looked up at him. 'I can't wait to meet him or her and be a mum.'

For some unaccountable reason Josh felt a lump in his throat. 'You'll be a great mum.'

'It'll be your turn next, Josh.' She slid her arm through his as they walked back through A and E. 'I'm working on it as we speak.'

If he'd been eating he would have choked. 'You're working on it?' He stopped dead, a suspicious frown in his eyes. 'What's that supposed to mean? What are you up to? What are you working on? Are you interfering again?'

'Me?' Louisa put a hand in the centre of her chest and looked innocent. 'Do I ever interfere?'

'Constantly.' They reached the ambulance bay and Josh pushed open the doors. 'Don't mess with my love life,' he warned, holding the door open so that she could walk through. 'I'm happy with it the way it is.'

'That's because you don't know any better.' Louisa walked past him, a shine in her eyes. 'But you're about to learn, Josh Sullivan, you're about to learn. Trust me on that one.'

Kat was *mortified*.

She'd missed an enormous fracture.

She'd been so wrapped up in Josh that she'd totally lost her powers of concentration.

Still thorougly embarrassed by the incident and wondering just how much Josh had guessed about her feelings, Kat watched as he examined the old lady on the trolley.

After the X-ray incident, as she now termed it, she'd seen a couple of patients by herself to restore her equilibrium and her confidence. She'd given advice on a simple case of sunburn and examined a badly sprained ankle. And when she'd finally felt she could look him in the eye again, she'd gone in search of Josh, only to find him moving Louisa's car.

'She's too pregnant to be driving this thing,' was all he'd said after he'd parked it neatly away from the ambulance bay and strode back into the department.

And now he was examining the old lady brought in by Louisa, and Kat watched him work in silent admiration. On the surface he seemed like the archetypal playboy, she mused, but there was much more to him than that. So much more depth.

He was gentle and reassuring and extremely thorough, asking a series of detailed questions as he conducted his examination.

Obviously he knew the patient and Kat wondered who she was.

'You seem dehydrated, Vera.' He straightened. 'The weather is very hot at the moment. Have you been drinking enough?'

'The dog's escaped,' Vera mumbled weakly, and Josh frowned and glanced at Hannah, the staff nurse, who gave a little shrug. 'Do you know where you are, Vera?'

'The dog escaped, you know,' the old lady fretted, plucking at the blanket with her fingers. 'I forgot to close the door.'

Hannah took her hand and gave it a squeeze. 'Don't you worry, Vera, everything will be fine.'

Josh looked at Vera, his gaze impassive. 'I'm going to run some tests, Vera, and see what they show.' He looked at Kat. 'Can you get a line in so that we can give her some fluids, and take bloods.' He listed the tests he wanted. 'I just need to make a couple of calls.'

Kat nodded and watched as he left the room. Then she turned her attention back to the patient.

'I don't want to have an accident. Have I had an accident?' Vera shifted on the trolley. 'Oh, I do hope not. It's so embarrassing.'

Something clicked in Kat's head. 'Vera, are you having trouble getting to the toilet on time?'

'No.' The old lady licked her lips, her mouth dry. 'I don't go much.'

'Right.' Kat asked a few more questions then gave Hannah a quick smile and slipped out of the room to look for Josh.

He was just finishing a phone call. 'I've called the medical reg. They're expecting her on the medical assessment unit. My guess is she has an infection.'

'Probably a kidney infection,' Kat said quickly, her cheeks slightly pink as she caught his quizzical gaze. 'In my opinion, she's been suffering from incontinence so to try and control it she's stopped drinking.'

Josh looked at her. 'You could be right. Makes sense, I suppose. Good thinking. We need to do a dipstick test on her urine.'

'Hannah is doing one now.'

Josh nodded and rubbed a hand over the back of his neck. 'All right. We'll transfer her up to the medical assessment unit and they can take it from there.' He walked back into the cubicle and explained to Vera what was happening even though she didn't seem to take any of it in. 'I'll tell Louisa and she can give Alice a ring, Vera. Don't worry about a thing. Hannah is going to take you upstairs now.'

Kat followed him out of the room. 'How do you know Vera? And who's Alice?'

'Her sister.' Josh strode towards the staffroom. 'They live next door to Mac. Louisa adopted them at Christmas. They were one of her projects.'

Kat laughed. 'Like Hopeful?'

'Nowhere near as troublesome as Hopeful,' Josh drawled, pushing open the door of the staffroom and stopping dead as he saw the number of people in there. 'I didn't know we were throwing a party.'

It seemed as though the entire staff had gathered to say hello to Louisa, and Kat felt something shift inside her.

What did it feel like to be part of a small community like this, where everyone not only knew their neighbours but cared for them? Where the staff all really minded when you left and wanted you to come back? What was it like to truly belong? For a moment she envied Louisa and then she pushed the thought away.

Her life was good. She didn't have anything to complain about.

She caught Louisa's gaze on her and forced a smile. 'Hello again.'

'Hi.' Louisa struggled to her feet and Josh strode forward and helped her.

'You weigh a ton and you're disrupting my department. Clear off, before I call the authorities and have you removed.'

Louisa smiled, unrepentant. 'It would take a crane to remove me now. How's Vera?' They moved to one side so that they couldn't be overheard.

'Kat thinks she has an infection brought on by lack of fluid. She's dehydrated.' Josh frowned. 'Do you know if she has a problem with incontinence?'

'Alice, her sister, would know.' Louisa looked at Kat. 'You think she's restricting her drinking?'

'I think it's possible,' Kat said, and Louisa nodded thoughtfully.

'Could be. Smart thinking. Well...' Her brow cleared. 'To be honest, it would be a relief if it was that and nothing worse. I'll pack her off to the GP once she's home and better. She can talk to him about the options. And holding off on the fluid isn't going to be one of them.'

Josh smiled at Kat. 'You can safely rely on my sister-in-law to interfere until it's sorted out,' he said mildly. 'Interfering is her special talent.'

'Come to lunch on Sunday,' Louisa said impulsively, catching Kat by the arm. 'I owe you a whole string of sausages after what happened the other day.'

'Oh!' taken by surprise Kat just stared at her. 'Well, I'm not sure. I—'

'Say yes,' Josh advised. 'She makes a barbecue sauce that's enough to bring a man to his knees.'

Kat hesitated. She was so unaccustomed to receiving social invitations that she didn't really know how to react. In her last post, everyone had worked together and then gone home and lived separate lives, often miles away from each other. She wasn't used to working as a member of such a close-knit team. Did she want to go? Did Louisa really want her? 'But I have Archie…'

'Well, of course you have Archie,' Louisa said happily, 'and he'll be a wonderful playmate for Hopeful. To be honest, he isn't the best dog to have around at a barbecue.'

'He isn't the best dog to have around at any culinary event,' Josh pointed out in a dry tone, and Louisa sighed.

'That is true. He does love his food. But most of all he loves other people's food.' She giggled and turned back to Kat. 'So will you come?'

Her smile was so genuine that Kat couldn't do anything but accept. 'All right. Thank you very much.'

'Twelve o'clock and dress casually. Better bring something to swim in, too.' Louisa took a pad and pen out of her bag and scribbled a map. 'We're just down the beach from you. If you're feeling really decadent, you can just walk along the sand, otherwise you can take the more conventional route and use the road. See you there.'

CHAPTER FIVE

'WE'RE going to a barbecue? Truly?' Archie jumped up and down with excitement. 'On the *beach?*'

'Calm down, Arch! You're like a kangaroo, and it's in Louisa's garden, but I think that's right next to the beach.' Much as she was looking forward to the day, all she really wanted to do was sleep, Kat thought as she stuffed sun hats and cream into a brightly coloured shoulder bag.

She felt totally exhausted.

For the first time for as long as she could remember, she wasn't sleeping well. During the day—apart from the X-ray incident, which she was trying valiantly to forget—she managed to keep her thoughts pretty much under control. But the moment she slid between the sheets it was an entirely different matter. Her mind took on a life of its own. It didn't help whether her eyes were open or closed, the vision was still the same. Josh, with no shirt on. Josh, his bronzed skin gleaming under the sun, his muscles flexed as he worked on the boat, his hair gleaming, glossy black.

Josh, Josh, Josh. He crowded her thoughts until her body was so heated and shivery that no amount of night air could cool her down. She'd tried sleeping with the window open and the window closed. She'd counted sheep and every other animal she could think of. She'd reminded herself that she didn't date men. That she wasn't interested in men. Nothing worked. Her head was still full of Josh and she was exhausted.

Maybe she needed to work harder, she thought grimly as she zipped the bag and slung it over her shoulder. She obviously just wasn't tired enough. If she exhausted herself physically, then she'd stop thinking about sex and sleep.

It wasn't as if she was even that interested in sex!

Well, today she was going to run on the beach and swim in the sea and make sure that she was so physically worn out that not sleeping just wouldn't be an option.

She'd followed Louisa's instructions and had dressed casually in a pair of denim shorts teamed with her favourite cream strap top. 'Your job, Archie O'Brien, is to keep an eye on that dog,' she said sternly. 'Make sure he doesn't eat everyone's lunch.'

Archie grinned at the prospect. 'Will Josh be there?'

Kat froze in the middle of slipping her feet into a pair of flat sandals. The possibility hadn't even occurred to her. Why hadn't it occurred to her? 'I don't know.'

Oh, help—she sincerely hoped not. She was trying to put him out of her mind. She closed her eyes briefly. Please, no, she thought. Not Josh…not today.

And then she remembered that he was working. He'd generously given her the weekend off to be with Archie, but he himself had worked yesterday and she knew he was down for today as well.

Having convinced herself that there was no way he could possibly be at Louisa's, she had a shock when she walked into the garden and he was the first person she saw.

Stripped to the waist again, a bottle of beer in his hand, he was chatting to a tall, dark-haired man who Kat remembered vaguely from that first day on the beach and presumed to be his brother.

Josh noticed her arrive and broke off in mid-sentence, his blue eyes fixed on hers for end-less seconds. Then his gaze slid slowly down her body, lingering on every curve.

'Put your tongue away, Josh,' his brother suggested helpfully. 'It's hanging out.' He stepped forward and held out a hand, his smile friendly. 'I'm Mac Sullivan. You must be Kat. Good to meet you. I apologise for my brother. Manners and subtlety have never been part of his make-up but I expect you must know that by now.'

Kat took his hand, immediately remember-ing their encounter on the beach. 'Hello again. This is Archie.' Suddenly overwhelmed by the presence of so many adults, Archie shrank against her, his fingers clutching her shorts.

Josh dropped to his haunches and smiled at him. 'Well, if it isn't my little boat friend. You did a great job the other morning. That section you helped me with…' He shook his head in disbelief. 'It's better than the rest. You must have a really good technique.'

Distracted, Archie let go of Kat's shorts. 'Are you a pirate?'

Josh threw back his head and laughed aloud. 'Do I look like a pirate?'

Yes, Kat thought helplessly, her eyes drawn to the strong column of his throat, the dark stubble on his jaw and those wicked blue eyes. *You look exactly like a pirate.*

'It's just that there's a picture of a pirate who looks just like you at my summer camp,' Archie said solemnly, his eyes fixed on Josh's face. 'He's standing on the deck of his ship and he looks *really* cool.'

Mac groaned. '*Don't* tell my brother he looks cool.'

'Why not?' Josh arched an eyebrow in his brother's direction. 'I *am* cool. Seriously cool. Not that I expect you to know anything about that. You're heading for fatherhood and a peo-

ple carrier faster than a guy can say ''duck''.'
He winked at Archie. 'I'm not a pirate, but I
love the sea so maybe I should have been one.
Do you like the sea?'

'More than anything.'

Kat felt her heart twist as she looked at her
son. She really, really had to arrange for him
to go sailing.

'Josh?' Archie sounded breathless, his little
voice full of hope. 'If I can get my mum to
say yes, can I help you with the boat again?'

Josh looked at him, a thoughtful expression
on his handsome face. 'You know how to get
your mum to say yes to things?'

A smile flickered across the little boy's face
and he nodded. 'Mostly.'

'Is that a fact?' Josh glanced at Kat, a
wicked gleam in his blue eyes. 'Well, then, I
know who to come to for tuition in that direction. Yes, Archie.' His gaze returned to the
boy. 'If your mum agrees...' he shrugged care-
lessly '...then, yes, you can help me with the
boat again.'

Torn between gratitude that he'd made her
son feel at home and anxiety about potentially

seeing more of him, Kat found herself at a loss for words. He made her feel breathless and shaky and aware of every single feminine part of herself. 'Well…' She flushed slightly and brushed strands of her long hair out of her eyes. 'I don't—'

'Good.' Josh straightened, his eyes fixed on her hair. Then he sucked in a breath and smiled. 'That's settled, then.' He dragged his gaze back to Archie. 'I'm guessing you're too young for beer, am I right?'

Archie grinned with delight. 'I'm six years old. What do you think?'

'Archie!' Kat's tone was sharp and she looked at her son in shock. 'Manners!'

'Stupid of me.' Josh nodded and his eyes slid over the boy. 'Of course you're too young. It's just that you look so grown up.' He rubbed the dark stubble on his chin, his expression serious. 'So what do kids of your age drink these days? Educate me.' He glanced towards the cool box, which was filled to the brim with ice and bottles of beer. 'I think there's cola in there or you could try Louisa's lemonade. It's good. She makes it herself and everything she makes is pretty good.'

'I like lemonade.'

'Lemonade it is, then. Good choice.' Josh strolled over to the cool box and pulled out a bottle. 'Kat? What about you?'

She wished he was wearing more than just a pair of shorts. His upper body was bronzed and powerfully built and he had muscles in every place a man should have muscles. There was no getting away from it. Josh Sullivan had an amazing body and she was finding it harder and harder to look away.

'I'll have lemonade, too, please.' Maybe if she drank enough, it would cool her down. She wasn't used to thinking like this. She wasn't used to feeling like this. She—

'Here.' He pressed a chilled glass into her hand. 'Hot, isn't it?'

Something in his tone made her lift her gaze to his and she was instantly trapped. 'It's summer,' she croaked, and he gave a slow smile that was more than a little ironic.

'I wasn't talking about the weather, Kat.'

Instinctively she looked for Archie but he'd taken his lemonade and was now at the other side of the garden with Hopeful and Louisa, entirely at home and comfortable.

'He's fine.' Josh knocked the top off a cold beer. 'Stop hiding behind your child.'

'I'm not hiding.'

'Yes, you are.'

Her fingers tightened on the glass. 'Why would I be hiding?'

'I'm asking myself the same question.' He took a step closer to her, a wicked, sexy gleam in his blue eyes. 'And I'm coming up with all sorts of interesting answers, Kat. You look good, by the way. In fact you look amazing. Just as good as you did in your nightdress, and that is *really* saying something. I ought to tell you that I thoroughly approve of what you wear in bed.'

She felt her cheeks heat. So he *had* noticed. 'I— You— I woke up and found Archie missing.' She brushed her hair out of her eyes, thoroughly flustered. 'I didn't even think about what I was wearing.'

'I know.' The smile in his eyes faded, to be replaced by something more serious. 'All you thought about was Archie, wasn't it?'

'I love him.'

'He's a lucky boy.'

Was he? Kat glanced across to her son who was rolling on the grass with the dog, helpless with laughter and thoroughly enjoying himself. 'I try to give him a good life, but it's hard not to worry.'

'Because you're a single parent?'

She gave a wry smile and blew a strand of hair away from her face. 'Actually, I'd probably worry even if I was married,' she confessed. 'Worry is my middle name.'

'Because you're a devoted mother.' Josh raised his beer to his lips and drank. 'Is his father on the scene?'

She shook her head. 'No.' She kept her tone light even though just thinking about Archie's father was enough to turn bright sunshine to darkness. 'He didn't want the responsibility.'

And although she'd long since recovered from the hurt, her heart still ached for Archie.

He should have had a father who cared. Who wanted to be with him.

'So you handle it all on your own.' Josh looked at her keenly. 'That must be tough.'

'Actually, sometimes I think it's a lot easier than dealing with a grown-up relationship,' Kat said wearily, taking a sip of her lemonade. 'His father was far more work than Archie ever is. He's a really, really good boy and very good company.'

Josh glanced across at Archie. 'Why does he always wear his clothes inside out?'

Kat laughed. 'Because he insists on dressing himself every morning and he hasn't got the hang of which way the labels go. I'm not allowed to help. He's fiercely independent.'

'I wonder who he gets that from?' There was no missing the irony in his tone, and Kat smiled.

'I admit it, he has my genes. But I'm pleased about that. There's nothing wrong with being independent. And he and I have such a good time together.'

'Yes.' Josh looked at Archie. 'He has a very entertaining line in conversation. Surprising, really.'

She lifted an eyebrow. 'You don't like children much, do you, Dr Sullivan?'

'I admit to very little personal experience in that area,' Josh drawled, and Kat's gaze slid to Louisa's bump.

'But all that is about to change.'

'Yes.' Josh lifted the bottle to his lips and drank again. 'I'm about to become an uncle for the first time. I'm hoping someone will buy me a manual. I know something about the general components, having worked at the hospital, and I could definitely do an emergency repair job if needed, but anything else is going to be beyond me.'

In spite of herself, Kat laughed and felt herself start to relax. No matter how wary he made her feel, she liked his sense of humour. 'Well, Archie certainly likes you.'

'Because, apparently, I look like a pirate,' Josh reminded her with a glitter in his eyes, 'and I own a boat.'

She swallowed. 'Thank you for making him feel at home.'

'He's a nice boy.' Josh turned to look at her and the tension in the air suddenly rose several notches. 'I know I'm in danger of repeating myself,' he said softly, 'but you really do look fantastic.'

She coloured and looked down at herself, suddenly self-conscious. 'It's just a pair of shorts.'

He laughed. 'I wasn't talking about your clothes.' His voice was a sexy drawl and his smile was all male. 'I was talking about you. You've gone very pink. You're not used to receiving compliments, are you? Why's that? You must know you're incredibly beautiful.'

She stared at him and swallowed hard. 'I don't— I mean, I'm not...'

Beautiful? He thought she was beautiful? Her heart took off like a dog after a cat and she made a wild grab at her sanity. This man probably seduced women on a daily basis. She wasn't going to fall for his patter. 'Is that one of your lines?' She sounded breathless and he threw back his head and laughed.

'Ouch. You have a suspicious nature, Katriona O'Brien, do you know that?' There was a lazy, sexy look in his blue eyes that made her stomach roll over.

'Don't, Josh.'

'Don't what?'

'Don't look at me like that!'

'Why? Because of Archie?'

'Because of Archie, yes.' She looked away but it made no difference. She felt his gaze on her. Felt the powerful chemistry pulse between them and spread her hands in a helpless gesture. 'We both know it wouldn't work.'

His eyes dropped to her mouth and lingered. 'I think it would work very well.'

'No, it wouldn't! I have a child and you—' she broke off and bit her lip.

'I what?' His gaze lifted to hers. 'I what, Kat?'

She sighed. 'We have different priorities, Josh, and you have to know enough about me by now to know that I would never do anything that might hurt Archie.'

Actually, at that precise moment she wasn't sure that their priorities were that different, but she wasn't about to share that thought with him.

If she put some distance between them and filled her mind with something else, then she could get herself back under control, she knew she could. As long as she didn't look at him. *As long as he put a shirt on.* And maybe he should shave, too. There was something wickedly attractive about his roughened jaw.

Pirate.

Thoroughly flustered, she took several steps backwards. 'I'm not looking for a relationship, Josh.' She felt breathless and lightheaded under his searching gaze.

'You may not have been looking,' he murmured, raising the bottle of beer to his lips again, 'but I have a feeling you might have just found one, angel.'

His soft endearment made her breath hitch in her throat and she took another step backwards. 'I'm going to help Louisa with the barbecue.' Without giving him a chance to answer, she turned and virtually sprinted across the grass to where Louisa was carefully laying pieces of chicken on the barbecue.

'This is my secret recipe for barbecue chicken.' She cast a smile in Kat's direction. 'It's quite spicy. I hope you like it. Are you all right? Your face is pink. Maybe you should wear a hat.'

Kat lifted a hand to her cheek, relieved that Louisa hadn't sensed the tense atmosphere between her and Josh. 'It is a little warm.' But she knew that if she was pink it had nothing to do with the heat of the August sunshine and everything to do with the way Josh made her feel.

Like a woman.

Like an attractive woman.

And she wasn't used to feeling that way. She bit her lip and passed Louisa a plate. She was used to feeling like a doctor. She was used to feeling like a mother. But she wasn't used to feeling like a woman.

'You've got time for a swim if you want one.' Louisa placed more chicken on the barbecue and Archie came sprinting up to them.

'Can we swim, Mum? Please? I'm boiled and so is Hopeful.'

The prospect of swimming had seemed very appealing when she'd woken that morning and seen the sunshine. But that had been before she'd discovered that Josh was present. Wherever she went she was aware of his gaze lingering on her, and her body was rapidly reaching boiling point. What was the matter with her? she wondered desperately. She *never* thought about sex and suddenly she could think about nothing else. It was just because she'd denied herself for so long, she reasoned, determined to apply logic to the situation. She just needed something to take her mind off Josh, and who better to do that than her son?

She smiled at him. 'All right, let's go swimming.'

Cold water. Lots of it. And physical activity. Surely that *had* to be a good thing.

Archie gave a whoop of excitement and immediately struggled out of his shorts and T-shirt, dropping them with careless abandon on the grass.

Louisa smiled indulgently. 'He's gorgeous, Kat, you're so lucky. Josh...' She waved a spatula at her brother-in-law. 'Go with them and do your lifeguard bit. They should avoid that area round the rocks. The currents are deadly.'

Kat glanced at her in dismay. She didn't want Josh to go with them. It was the last thing she wanted. 'We'll be fine, honestly, we don't need—'

'Josh will go with you,' Louisa said firmly. 'We don't want any accidents. I'm not as nimble as I used to be.'

Everyone laughed and suddenly Kat remembered what Josh had said about Louisa interfering and matchmaking. Was she up to something? She looked at the other woman suspiciously but Louisa was concentrating hard on turning the chicken, her expression innocent.

Kat relaxed. Of course Louisa wasn't up to anything. She was just a naturally kind, caring woman. She obviously hadn't sensed the chemistry between Kat and Josh and therefore hadn't recognised that Kat was trying to put distance between them.

And Josh was already wearing a pair of surf shorts so he'd clearly intended to swim at some point during the day.

Horribly self-conscious, Kat stripped down to the emerald green swimsuit she was wearing under her shorts. He saw millions of women on the beach every day, she reminded herself, gritting her teeth and telling herself not to be so ridiculous. If she ignored him, he'd soon lose interest.

And then her life could get back to normal.

She could forget about Josh.

They could work together as colleagues and nothing more.

It was going to be fine.

Josh followed Archie and Kat into the sea at a safe distance, making a mental note to have a stern word with Louisa when Kat wasn't around. The girl was up to her tricks again. Not that he'd objected to the idea of a swim, but he liked to be in control of his own love life and he certainly didn't want Louisa's help, no matter how sweet and well meaning she was. From the moment Louisa had innocently suggested a swim he'd known what she was up to. Fortunately Kat seemed oblivious but, then, she didn't know Louisa as well as he did, he thought grimly.

And Kat was right, of course.

How could any relationship between them ever work? He never dated single mothers and, apart from his patients in A and E, he'd never spent any time with a child in his life.

Josh dragged a hand through his hair and squinted into the sun, watching from the water's edge as they plunged into the water, gasping and shrieking as the cold waves closed around their legs for the first time.

Why did she have to be so beautiful?

But he knew it was so much more than that. Kat was clever and sharp and she challenged his mind.

But she had Archie, he reminded himself firmly. And that made all the difference. Josh cursed softly. He was nobody's idea of a father figure, that was for sure. He didn't want that responsibility.

Not that the boy wasn't sweet, because actually he was. Josh's eyes narrowed as he watched the boy dive fearlessly into the water, his skinny arms and legs moving smoothly as he swam. Before he'd met Archie it had never crossed his mind that a child could be good company. But Archie was good company. And funny.

Josh gave himself a mental shake. Since when had he had anything at all in common with a six-year-old?

'Josh!' Archie's shout cut through his thoughts. 'Come in and swim.'

Unable to find a reason not to, Josh waded in, wincing slightly at the cold. 'This is bracing,' he muttered to Kat, and she laughed, not quite meeting his eyes.

He'd already sensed that she wasn't used to flirting with men. Had there been no one in her life since Archie's father?

Suddenly he wanted to ask, wanted to know everything about her. He, who preferred to keep his relationships light-hearted and superficial.

What the hell was happening to him?

'English sea, Josh.' She looked at him then, her eyes challenging as she dipped her shoulders under the surface. She rose, gasping, her hair falling sleek and wet past her shoulders. 'Oh, my goodness—that is truly freezing.' She laughed and he found himself captivated.

She looked like a mermaid. An extremely beautiful mermaid. And those amazing green eyes were enough to bewitch a man into doing something stupid. Like forgetting that he didn't date single mothers.

He swallowed and decided that cold water could only be a good thing in the circumstances. He dived under the water and surfaced next to a thoroughly over-excited Archie.

'You're a good swimmer.' He scraped a hand over his face to clear the water and smiled at the boy. 'Did you learn at school?'

Archie shook his head. 'My mum taught me. She thinks everyone should be able to swim.'

'Then your mum is a sensible lady.' Josh looked at her, watching as she swam up to them. He was trying hard not to notice just how good she looked in a swimsuit.

He tried to remind himself that Louisa was obviously matchmaking like mad and he tried to remind himself that Kat had a child.

Those things alone should have been enough to make him run fast and hard in the opposite direction.

In fact, there were so many reasons why he should back off he couldn't count them.

'Will you race me?' Archie tugged at Josh's arm, his expression excited. 'First person to Mum wins.'

Kat laughed and obligingly swam away from them to position herself as the finishing line. Josh watched her go and then looked back at Archie. What the hell was he supposed to do? What were the politics of swimming with a six-year-old? He didn't have the first clue. Was he supposed to lose? Or was that considered patronising? He didn't want to do the wrong thing.

'I get a start.' Archie waded in front of him, glancing over his shoulder at Josh who was still wondering how to play it.

'You get a start?'

'Of course.' The little boy grinned. 'Because I'm so much smaller than you. Otherwise it wouldn't be fair, would it?'

Josh felt a rush of relief and then wondered what was happening to him. He cared about Archie's feelings and the realisation shocked him. He'd never considered himself to be interested in children.

'I'll say ''go'',' Archie yelled, still wading forward, and Josh smiled.

'Hey!' His voice carried and he saw Kat listening. 'Isn't that far enough? Give me a chance!'

'Go!' Archie yelled with no warning at all, and ploughed forward at the same time, his arms and legs moving like windmills as he thrashed through the water towards his mother.

Josh diplomatically waited for a few seconds and then started a steady front crawl, keeping one eye on the child. He held himself one stroke behind the boy, hoping that was the right thing to do.

'I won, I won!' Archie was leaping around in the water, whooping with delight and Josh was amazed by how good it made him feel.

'I couldn't catch you!' He wiped the water from his eyes. 'What a swimmer you are!'

Kat was laughing and shaking her head. 'Not in the slightest bit competitive, my child, as you can see.' She picked Archie up and smiled at Josh, a curious look in her green eyes. 'That was sweet of you.'

She looked surprised, as if she hadn't expected him capable of considering the child's feelings, and he was forced to admit that he was pretty surprised himself.

Partly because the psychology of a child's mind wasn't his strong point and miraculously he seemed to have got it right, but mostly because he was having such a good time.

Usually, if there was a race, he only derived pleasure if he was the winner. It would never have occurred to him that he could have got such a high from seeing the boy's pleasure at winning.

'Can we do it again, Josh?' Archie was clearly ecstatic about his victory. 'This time I promise to give you a chance,' he offered generously, and Josh pulled a face, watching as the boy wriggled out of his mother's arms and waded forward to start the race again.

'Not sure if my ego can take being thrashed twice in one day.'

Kat laughed. 'Coward.' Drops of water clung to her dark lashes and her hair hung down her back. He noticed that it was much darker when it was wet and he also noticed that her swimsuit revealed every line and curve of her body. Suddenly Josh forgot about Archie. He forgot everything except the woman standing in front of him.

Her laughter faded and he saw uncertainty flicker in her eyes as the look in her eyes reflected his own. 'Josh…'

The urge to lean forward and kiss her soft mouth was almost overwhelming. He wanted to touch and taste. *He wanted to take—*

A flash of animal lust shot through him and he turned away with a soft curse, reminding himself of all the reasons why this was *not* a good idea.

'Josh!'

With something approaching relief he turned his attention back to Archie, who was yelling his name.

Cold water.

He needed seriously cold water.

Dipping under the surface, he swam underwater until he reached the boy. 'Do you really want to race again?' The trouble was, this time he didn't want to hold back. He was pumped up and almost bursting with frustration and what he really needed was a burst of intense physical activity to calm his libido. 'I've got an idea.'

'What?'

'I'll race against your mum and you can be the finishing post.'

Archie nodded enthusiastically. 'Mum!' he shouted, and bounced in the water. 'I'll wade over there and you and Josh can swim to me.' He started off and Kat frowned.

'No, Arch, not on your own. You're not a strong enough swimmer.'

Josh swore softly. 'I'm sorry, I didn't think of that.'

'I'm probably just being paranoid—you know me and worry.' Kat swam quickly after her son and Josh let out a long breath.

What did he think he was doing? One small success and suddenly he thought he knew everything there was to know about children.

Hardly!

He had absolutely no idea what they could do at different ages, as he'd just proved. Left to his care, Archie probably would have drowned.

Suddenly furious with himself, he waited until Kat had reached Archie and once he'd satisfied himself that she had the child and his responsibility had ended, he turned and ploughed into the waves, swimming out to sea with a powerful front crawl.

He swam until his shoulders ached and his eyes stung from the salt. Until his lungs shrieked for air and his legs felt leaden. He swam until his mind was calmer and his body should have felt soothed.

But it didn't.

Finally he gave up and returned to the beach to find his brother standing on the shore. There was no sign of Kat or the boy.

'Thought you were swimming across to France,' Mac said mildly, handing Josh a towel. 'Glad you changed your mind. Louisa's made enough food for an army.'

Josh took the towel. 'You need to tell that wife of yours to stop matchmaking.' He dried his face and slung the towel round his shoulders. 'I can arrange my love life without her help.'

And he didn't want her driving Kat in the opposite direction.

'Is she helping? Oh, dear.' Mac turned to walk back towards the house and Josh fell into step. 'That's the end of you, then.'

Josh glared. 'The woman interferes!'

'Well, I know that.' Mac stifled a yawn. 'If she didn't interfere, we wouldn't be married now, as you well know. And if you hadn't also interfered, I never would have met her.'

Josh kicked the sand moodily. 'I don't interfere.'

'You arranged for Louisa to move in with me last Christmas,' Mac reminded him dryly. 'If that's not interfering, I don't know what is.'

'That's entirely different. I just knew you were right for each other.'

'Kat's not right for you?'

Josh thought of her green eyes and lush curves. He thought of her sharp brain and her quick tongue. 'She's fine.'

'But?'

He looked at his brother. 'I don't mess with single mothers.'

'So?' Mac shrugged as if the problem had a simple solution. 'Don't mess with her, then. Take it seriously. For the first time in your life take a relationship further. Who knows? You might find that you like it.'

Josh stopped as though he'd been shot. Suddenly he felt as though he was suffocating. Take a relationship further? He never took relationships further, and that was when women had no ties. Kat had ties. She had Archie. What about Archie? The responsibility stifled him.

'No.' He shook his head and ran a hand over the back of his neck. He was sweating. It was the heat, he decided. Just the heat. 'It's too complicated. The risk is too great.' He thought of Archie's huge smile. 'And I'm not about to upset a child.'

'Well, that's good to hear, but can you walk and talk?' Mac jerked his head towards the house. 'We need to get going if you want to eat this side of Christmas. That's why I came to get you. When Kat and Archie reappeared without you, Louisa thought you'd drowned. And I don't see why you're so freaked out. The fact that you care about upsetting a child has to be good. It means you care about him. It means there's hope for you.' He slapped his brother on the shoulder. 'You might even make a half-decent uncle with a bit of training.'

Josh stared at Mac. How could he care about Archie? *He was just a kid.*

But he already did care about him and the realisation stunned him. He'd never had a relationship with a child before.

Mac sighed. 'Josh, get a grip. And wipe that soppy, distracted look off your face or you'll never hear the last of it from Louisa and neither will I. She's already choosing her hat for the wedding.'

The word 'wedding' exploded like a bucket of cold water over his head and Josh blinked.

Of course, that would be exactly what a woman like Kat would expect. A wedding. And he wasn't the marrying kind.

There were other women with curves and green eyes, he reminded himself firmly as he strode off through the dunes towards his brother's house. Other women with brains. Women who didn't come with more baggage than a jumbo jet.

And the only way to be totally sure that he wouldn't hurt Archie was to find one of them. Quickly.

The food was delicious.

Kat supervised as Archie filled his plate and then went to sit on the rug that Louisa had placed in the shade.

'Don't let Hopeful eat your sausages,' she warned as she dropped a kiss on his head. 'This time they're for you.'

'That dog has already eaten loads,' Louisa grumbled, adding dressing to a huge green salad and lifting a bowl of shiny black olives. 'Help yourselves, everyone. Not you, Hopeful.' She tried to grab the dog but he dodged her and bounded over to Archie, who waved a finger at him sternly.

'Sit.'

Hopeful sat.

Four adults stared in astonishment.

Playing to his audience, Archie looked at the dog. 'Lie down.'

Hopeful lay down, his head resting on his paws.

Louisa made a sound in her throat and Mac laughed. 'Finally, that dog listens to someone. Looks as though we can cancel the hearing test, Lu.'

'It's amazing.' Louisa tilted her head on one side and watched as Hopeful lay at the boy's feet, gazing up at him. 'He never, *ever* does as he's told. Archie, you obviously have the knack.'

Archie munched his sausage and basked in the praise.

'Maybe he likes children,' Kat suggested, and Louisa patted her rounded stomach.

'I really hope so. He's going to be my babysitter.'

Mac rolled his eyes. 'I can't believe I'm hearing this. That dog isn't going anywhere near the baby—we'd better get that straight right now.'

Josh helped himself to food and Kat concentrated her attentions on her own plate. She was trying so hard not to look at him that her body was aching with the tension.

Since he'd returned from the beach with Mac he hadn't glanced once in her direction. And she hadn't glanced at him. But she felt him. With every bone in her body, she felt him.

When he'd swum out to sea, she'd understood exactly what he'd been doing.

He was putting as much distance between them as possible, as if the few moments of fun they'd had together had placed an intolerable strain on his bachelor genes.

She bit her lip. He'd been fine until Archie had asked him to race. Which meant it was Archie who was the problem.

Impatient with herself, she sighed. Well, of course it was Archie. Why did that come as a surprise? A man like Josh didn't want to spend his day with a child. Or with a woman who worried about her child. He was used to women who worried about their hair and their nails and what they were going to wear. She never had time to afford more than a cursory glance at her appearance. And when she was with Archie she was just pleased if she got through the day without wearing ketchup.

All right, so there was chemistry between them but a relationship needed more than chemistry to make it work.

She watched Archie discreetly feed a sausage to the dog and felt a twinge of sadness. Things could have been so different and it would have been wonderful to share the load with a man who shared her strong belief in family.

But unfortunately Paul had only believed in himself.

'He's a lovely boy.' Louisa followed her gaze. 'Am I allowed to ask what happened to his father?'

'He wasn't interested in Archie.' Kat's tone was flat. 'We don't see him. But it's hard. Archie is getting to that age where he notices differences, and he's starting to ask about his dad.'

'Hmm.' Louisa looked at her thoughtfully. 'And what do you say?'

'That relationships don't always work out.' Kat nibbled her chicken. 'That families aren't always a mummy, daddy and two children. The usual sort of stuff that you say to justify being on your own.' She looked at Mac and Josh. 'You're so lucky, being part of this family.'

Josh might be a confirmed bachelor, but there was no doubting his strong attachment to his brother and Louisa. And she was sure that if there was anything he needed to learn about being an uncle, he'd learn it.

'I know how lucky I am.' Louisa's tone was soft. 'I'd been looking for the right family to join for a long time. The Sullivans are nearly perfect.'

Kat looked at her. 'You were looking for a family to join? What do you mean by that?'

Louisa helped herself to more chicken. 'Didn't manage it as a child so I always promised myself that when I grew up, I'd find the right people. I was a homeless waif,' she confessed. 'I spent my childhood in foster-homes and in care. Too much of a handful for anyone to want to adopt me. Maybe that's why I identify with Hopeful.' She glanced at the dog who was now sprawled over Archie's legs like a blanket. 'I know what it's like to be a misfit.'

Kat couldn't hide her surprise. 'I— You were in care?'

She found it impossible to believe.

'Close your mouth, you're about to swallow a fly,' Louisa teased. 'What's wrong?'

Kat struggled to put her thoughts into words. 'It's just that you seem so…happy. And yet you obviously had a really difficult childhood.'

'It was the pits.' Shadows flickered across Louisa's face but then faded, blotted out by her smile. 'But I always told myself that the past didn't matter, only my future. And I was determined not to let the before spoil my happy-ever-after, if you see what I mean. I knew what I wanted. To belong. And now I do. And, yes, I know I'm lucky.'

Kat glanced across the garden to Mac, who was talking to his brother with one eye on his wife.

'He adores you.'

'I know.' Louisa gave him a loving smile then turned her attention back to Kat. 'And what about you?'

Kat didn't pretend to misunderstand her. 'I have Archie.'

'And he's great. But you should share him with someone.' Louisa chuckled as Archie rolled on the rug with the dog. 'It's selfish of you to keep a gorgeous boy like that to yourself.'

'Unfortunately, real life isn't that straightforward.' Kat couldn't keep the sadness out of her tone. 'I haven't yet met a man capable of living up to the responsibility of his own child, let alone someone else's. And I wouldn't ever take a risk on Archie's happiness.'

'Life is all about taking risk,' Louisa said thoughtfully. 'It's just important to take the right risk at the right time, and you'd need a special man to make you do it, I can see that.'

'I'm not looking for a man,' Kat said hastily, wondering if Louisa had intercepted the chemistry sizzling between her and Josh. 'Although sometimes I think Archie needs more of a male influence in his life. He's such a *boy* boy, if you know what I mean.'

Louisa licked barbecue sauce from her fingers and smiled. 'I can see that about him. He's very rough and tumble.'

'And he loves things like football—' Kat broke off and brushed her hair out of her eyes with a rueful smile. 'I'm not much of a footballer but I do my best.'

'Josh is a great footballer. He'd kick a ball around with Archie.'

Kat shot her a suspicious look but Louisa's expression was totally innocent as she put her plate down on the table.

'Hey, Archie!' She called across, laughter in her eyes. 'That dog of mine is getting fat and lazy. Fancy playing football with him?'

'Really? He can play football?' Archie scrambled to his feet and Hopeful bounded around him, tail wagging.

'He's brilliant in goal.' Louisa rubbed her back and winced. 'There's a ball here somewhere.' She glanced over at Mac. 'Where's the football? I know I saw it the other day.'

He grinned and dropped his eyes to her stomach. 'You look as though you might very possibly have swallowed it, my sweetheart.'

'Oh, ha, ha, very funny.' Louisa walked awkwardly across the lawn towards him but her eyes were dancing. 'The jokes are on me now, but pretty soon the tables will be turned, Dr Sullivan. This particular football is going to be keeping you awake at nights.'

'Don't remind me,' Mac groaned, but there was no missing the love in his eyes as he looked at his wife.

Josh placed a hand on Louisa's abdomen. 'It's so enormous. I know I keep asking you this, but doesn't it hurt?'

'Only when he kicks me hard. Like now.' Louisa winced. 'How are you two at delivering babies?'

'Don't even joke about it.' Josh gave a shudder and backed away, hands raised in a gesture of male helplessness. 'I'm an A and E doctor. I don't deliver babies.'

'A and E doctors are *supposed* to be able do everything,' Louisa reminded him mildly, and Josh shook his head, but there was laughter in his eyes.

'Not babies! I'll do anything except babies. Fall over and break all your bones and I'm definitely your man, but babies…' He shivered dramatically. 'Kat did obstetrics last, she can deliver it.'

They all laughed and Kat tried to join in, but she felt strangely heavy inside. They were a wonderful family and spending the day with them reminded her of how lonely her life was.

Kat gave herself a shake and watched as the two men chased around the garden, kicking the football to her little boy, who whooped and sprinted after it.

He was in boy heaven.

'Hopeful goes in goal,' Louisa yelled, gesturing to two ancient apple trees laden with fruit. 'Goal is between those two trees. But don't slip on the apples.'

They played for the rest of the afternoon until Archie tripped over the ball and started to cry.

'He's tired,' Kat said quickly, scooping him up into her arms and giving him a cuddle. She checked her watch and gave a gasp. 'I didn't realise it was so late! I need to get him home to bed. Thank you so much for a wonderful day.'

'It was wonderful having you.' Louisa beamed at her. 'Josh will walk you home.'

'What?' Josh looked as though she'd suggested he walk naked down the high street. 'Walk her home?'

'Yes.' Louisa's tone was patient as she cleared the last of the plates. 'Just in case she gets mugged.'

'Mugged?' Kat blinked. 'But it's still light and I only live over there.'

'Two girls were mugged on the beach just last week,' Louisa said, looking at Josh with a stern look in her eyes. 'You live right next door to her so it makes absolute sense for you to walk home together.'

Josh frowned, a flicker of annoyance in his eyes. 'Louisa...'

'I won't get mugged.' Kat took one look at the dangerous look in Josh's eyes and felt a cloud descend on her. It was so obvious that he didn't relish the idea of walking home with her, and who could blame him? He obviously had other plans for his evening. Undoubtedly something much more exciting than acting as a bodyguard for a woman and her child.

And he hadn't so much as glanced in her direction since that episode in the sea.

She quickly gathered up their things that were scattered across the lawn and said her farewells to Mac.

Josh was standing by the gate. Holding tightly to Archie's hand, she swung the bag over her shoulder and gave him a cool look.

'You don't have to take me home.'

He didn't quite meet her eyes. 'Louisa's right. It makes sense,' he muttered, reaching for her bag.

She held onto it. 'I can carry my own bag,' she snapped, and he blinked at her.

'I thought it might be heavy.'

'Well, I could carry it even if it was heavy.' She shot him a look of intense irritation. 'Since the day Archie was born I've been lugging pushchairs and car seats and one increasingly heavy child. I can carry a beach bag.'

This time he did look at her and there was a question mixed with the wariness. 'All right.' There was a gleam in his eyes. 'If you're Miss Muscle, you can carry my bag.' He handed her an overstuffed sports bag and despite her best efforts a giggle escaped. He had a way of making her laugh even when she was determined to be angry with him.

'Weedy, that's your problem.' He had muscles that drew the female eye and weedy was about the one thing he most certainly was not. 'You don't need to walk me home, Josh.'

She had too much pride to allow him to do it.

She was too independent.

'Indulge me.' He glanced over her shoulder. 'I'm scared of my sister-in-law. If anything untoward were to happen to you, I'd never hear the last of it.'

'We both know I'm not going to get mugged.'

'No, but I will if I don't escort you.' His tone was dry. 'Have you ever tried arguing with Louisa? Trust me, it doesn't work. Especially when she's interfering.'

'How is she interfering?' It seemed to Kat that she was just being caring, but she didn't have time to explore that further with Josh because Archie was whining and tugging at her hand impatiently, not understanding the delay.

'When are we going? I'm bored. I want to go home.'

He wasn't really bored, of course, he was tired and he needed to go to bed.

She made her decision. 'Come on, then.' It was quicker than arguing and it wasn't as if it was far, she reasoned. And it wasn't as if she was making Josh go out of his way. He lived right next door.

Archie took all her attention on the way home. First he wanted to walk. Then he wanted to be carried. And he whined and moaned and generally made a fuss.

Josh frowned as she scooped him into her arms for the second time. 'He's too heavy for you.'

'I'm used to carrying him if he gets tired. I always carry him.'

'Well, you shouldn't.' He looked at Archie. 'Aren't you big enough to walk?'

Archie buried his head in Kat's shoulder. 'I'm tired.'

'Too much running around. Fancy a ride on my shoulders?' He angled his head. 'The view is probably better higher up.'

Archie's face lit up and he stretched out his arms, making it impossible for Kat to refuse.

'There.' Josh lifted him easily and hitched him onto his shoulders, holding firmly onto the little boy's legs. 'How's that?'

'Cool.' Archie gazed upwards. 'I'm quite close to the moon. Did you know Neil Armstrong was the first man on the moon?'

Josh looked at Kat, astonishment in his eyes. 'Do kids his age know things like that?'

'Of course we do,' Archie said scathingly. 'We're learning about it in summer camp. The planets. Mars, Jupiter, Pluto...' He curled his fingers into Josh's hair to keep his balance, and Josh winced.

Kat struggled not to laugh. 'Don't grab his hair, Arch,' she said quickly, reaching on tip-toe to unclasp her son's hands. 'He's got your legs, you're quite safe. Just hold his head gently—that's it.'

They arrived outside her door and Josh reached up and lifted Archie down from his shoulders with effortless ease while Kat watched. Something twisted inside her. She couldn't put Archie on her shoulders, he was too heavy. And she'd never be able to lift him like that.

'OK—well, here we are.' She smiled at Archie. 'Say bye to Josh.'

'Bye, Josh, and thanks for the ride.' Archie shot up to the front door, suddenly eager to see his toys, and Kat was left alone with Josh.

For some reason she suddenly felt hideously shy. 'Right then…' She gave him an awkward smile. 'This is me, so…' she waved a hand, '…I'll say goodnight.'

He hesitated and glanced towards the door, and for a wild moment she thought he was going to suggest that he come in for coffee.

But then he gave a brief smile and a nod, shifted his sports bag on his shoulder and made off down the road without a backward glance.

Kat walked up the path to her cottage and unlocked the door.

Sunday night.

She'd bath Archie, read him a story and then settle down with her A and E textbook. And if that was a slightly sad way for a twenty-seven-year-old to spend a Sunday evening, she wasn't going to think about it.

And she wasn't—*she definitely wasn't*—going to think about Josh Sullivan.

CHAPTER SIX

THE following week was a nightmare.

Kat hadn't thought it possible to be so distracted by a man. Since her disastrous relationship with Archie's father, she'd had no trouble at all in keeping men at a distance. She barely noticed them as anything other than friends and colleagues.

But it would have been impossible not to notice Josh. Everything about him was designed to be noticed. The glossy dark hair, the laughing blue eyes that teased and hinted at no end of wicked thoughts, the bold pirate's smile designed to turn a woman inside out. And then there was his body, of course. Kat clutched the notes she was holding to her chest and tried valiantly to blot out the image. Maybe if she'd met him in the winter things would have been different. Maybe then he wouldn't have been half-undressed all the time and she wouldn't have had such a clear image of strong male shoulders and lean muscular legs.

She shook herself.

This was ridiculous.

She was behaving like a teenager with a stupid crush and she needed to snap out of it. And if her wretched body had suddenly woken up—she lifted her chin in a determined gesture—well, it could just go straight back to sleep again.

'Who can just go straight back to sleep again?' Josh strolled up to her and lifted an eyebrow.

Kat gaped at him. Had she spoken aloud? 'I—I—must have been thinking aloud.'

'Right. Archie having problems sleeping?'

Not Archie.

Kat dropped the notes she was holding and inevitably they scattered over the floor. With a soft curse she dropped to her knees and gathered the various papers together with shaking hands. 'Did you want something?' Thoroughly flustered, she stuffed the pages back in the folder and scrambled to her feet. 'You were obviously looking for me.'

'Yes.' His eyes dropped to her mouth. 'I was.'

She really, *really* wished he wouldn't look at her like that.

She licked her lips and clutched the notes tightly. It was that or drop them again. 'So, what did you want?'

'You.' His gaze lifted and he gave a slow, sexy smile. 'I wanted you, Kat.'

Her knees shook, her heart raced and she desperately wanted to look away from that smile. But she couldn't. Her gaze was fastened to his and she watched his smile fade. Watched a very different emotion flicker into his eyes.

And then the doors to Resus crashed open behind them.

'You're both hiding in here.' Hannah hurried across the room, looking harassed. 'That's good. The paramedics are bringing in a collapsed teenager who was on holiday with some friends.'

Kat dragged her gaze away from Josh and felt the burn in her cheeks. 'Another drug incident, do you think?' Her tone was calm and professional and she busied herself at the intubation tray, hoping that Hannah wouldn't notice anything amiss.

'No idea.' Hannah quickly checked the necessary equipment. 'So far no real clues. Could be something as simple as food poisoning from the description. Maybe she ate some dodgy seafood on the beach.'

The paramedics arrived moments later, with the teenager groaning and clutching her stomach.

'She's been sick all the way in the ambulance and complaining of pains in her stomach,' the paramedic said, giving a full brief to Josh as they transferred the girl across from the stretcher to the trolley.

'Acute abdomen?' Kat glanced at Josh and he narrowed his eyes.

'Possibly.'

Which meant he thought it was something different. Kat loved watching him work. He was like a detective, searching for clues and missing nothing.

'I'm so thirsty…' The girl gave a groan and wretched again while Hannah handed her a clean bowl and made sympathetic noises.

'You're thirsty because you're sick,' she said soothingly, and Josh frowned.

'Or maybe not.' His tone was thoughtful. 'Maybe she's thirsty for an entirely different reason. Let's get a blood pressure and pulse reading.' He drew closer to the girl, watching the rise and fall of her chest as she breathed in and out heavily. 'Dr O'Brien, what do you know about Küssmaul respiration?'

Kat racked her brains, mentally leafing through the various chapters of her A and E textbook. Then something clicked into place. 'My first medical house job.' She looked at him. 'We had a diabetic man on the ward and he—' She broke off and looked at the girl. 'You think that's what's wrong here?'

'Her breath smells of ketones.' He shrugged. 'Could be.'

'And the GI symptoms?'

'They're common in a hyperglycaemic crisis and they're often misdiagnosed.'

But not in his department, Kat thought, filled with silent admiration for his skills. He didn't miss anything and he always looked beyond the obvious.

'Check her BMG and her urine for glucose and ketones,' he instructed, and one of the other nurses did as he requested while Hannah checked the girl's blood pressure and pulse.

Josh scanned the machine with a nod. 'Hypotensive and tachycardic. I'm pretty sure that we're looking at a case of diabetic ketoacidosis. It would fit her signs and symptoms.' He tried talking to the girl but her answers were incoherent and gave them no clues at all. Josh gave up. 'Hannah…' He glanced up, his expression urgent. 'Can you get someone to talk to the friends? We need some history here. Is she an uncontrolled diabetic? There are no marks on her skin so it doesn't look as though she's been injecting. I need everything they have on her medical history.'

'I'll get some details from them.' Hannah vanished from the room and Josh looked at Kat.

'Let's get an IV in and an infusion of saline started. If that hypotension persists then we might need to increase the rate and switch to colloids.'

Moments later Hannah was back in the room. 'They say that she isn't a diabetic but she's been behaving oddly for the past couple of days. They thought she had a bug.'

'Diabetic ketoacidosis can develop over several days in younger, undiagnosed diabetics.'

Kat slid a venflon into the vein. 'What blood tests do you want?'

Josh's eyes flashed a challenge. 'What do you think, Dr Sullivan?'

'Blood glucose obviously.' Quickly she selected the right bottle. 'U&Es, creatinine, osmolality…' She listed the others and Josh gave a nod.

'And a full blood count and arterial blood gases. Let's send off blood cultures and get an ECG done. And call the radiologists. I want a chest X-ray.'

Kat finished taking the blood and labelled the bottles. 'Do you think she has an infection?'

'I think it's possible. We'll send a sample of her urine for microscopy and culture and do a throat swab.' Josh checked her plasma glucose level. 'All right, folks, let's give her

20 units of insulin to start with, and then we need to monitor that level every hour. Has someone called the medical reg? Obviously she's going to need to be admitted.'

Hannah nodded. 'He's on his way. He's already in the department actually, so he'll be along in a minute.'

They worked until the girl was stable and then handed her over to the medical team. 'I'll take her up to the ward and then I'll come back and sort this place out,' Hannah said, glancing around Resus with a rueful expression on her face. 'What a mess.'

With the help of a porter, she guided the trolley through the doors and they swung shut behind her.

Silence descended on the room.

Kat swallowed. Suddenly it was just the two of them again. 'That was a really interesting case.' She kept her voice bright and professional. 'I love the way you always think laterally. You see abdominal pain but you don't automatically think acute surgical abdomen. You always manage to—'

'Kat.' Josh interrupted her in a soft tone. 'You're chattering. What the hell's the matter with you?'

He was the matter with her!

'You were good, that's all,' she said gruffly, and there was a long silence. A silence that made her so uncomfortable that she turned away and concentrated on restocking Resus. As far as she knew, there was no substitute for work when it came to taking your mind off a problem.

And Josh Sullivan was definitely becoming a problem. *A big problem.*

Reaching for a new bag of saline, she ripped off the protective cover and attached a giving set. Then she did the same with a bag of dextrose, aware that Josh was just lounging against one of the low cupboards, watching her.

She became more and more flustered and turned her attention to the intubation tray. She snapped open laryngoscopes to check the bulbs; she counted ET tubes and checked tapes.

Then she was forced to go into his cupboard. 'Excuse me.' She moved closer to him and then realised her mistake. It was like stepping into a force field, programmed to draw her in.

She felt the brush of his arm against hers, the warmth of his breath, and for a microsecond she stilled, feeling the shock waves pulse through her sensitised body.

And then he moved.

Swiftly and without hesitation he hauled her against him, turning her so that she was pressed against the cupboard, giving her no option of escape.

But she didn't want to escape. They'd been building towards this from the first second their eyes had met on the beach, and the moment his mouth crashed down on hers she was lost. The heat that had been building consumed her, the sudden blaze of passion burning through reason and resolve.

Without lifting his mouth, his fingers found the hem of her top and he jerked it upwards, his hand sliding, searching until it closed over one breast. The ache between her thighs rose to almost intolerable levels and she pressed against him, squirming to get closer and closer, feeling him rock hard and male through the thin fabric of his scrub suit.

Oh, God, how had she done without this for so long?

But the answer was immediately clear in her head. Because she'd never had this. Never once in the past had she ever felt this desperate, almost animal urgency to be with a man. Never once had she wanted a man the way she wanted Josh.

She felt the skilful sweep of his tongue and responded instantly, matching his greed with her own frantic urgency. There was no holding back. She wanted, *needed,* every bit as much as he clearly did.

'Kat…' He groaned her name and slid a hand down the back of her scrub suit, his fingers seeking and finding.

She cried out at the intimacy of his touch and clutched at his shoulders, her whole body shivering and trembling against his as excitement consumed her. His touch was wickedly good and she felt the heat build low in her pelvis.

He dragged his mouth from hers with obvious difficulty, his breathing uneven and his blue eyes hazy as his hands returned to her waist. 'We can't do this here. We need to find a room with a lock.'

She stared at him stupidly. A lock?

And then reality descended on her with all the brutality of a cold shower. Her eyes shifted from his handsome face, from the heat burning in his blue eyes and took in the bright lights, the metal and chrome and the sheer starkness of their surroundings.

They were in Resus and they'd all but made love on the trolley.

She closed her eyes, appalled and totally embarrassed.

What had happened to both of them? Neither of them had given any thought to their surroundings, to the fact that anyone could have come in and caught them. She gave a whimper of horror at the thought of what might have happened.

How could she have allowed it?

She squirmed with mortification as she acknowledged the truth. That she hadn't just allowed it, *she'd encouraged it.*

'This is crazy.' She dragged herself out of his arms, wondering why it felt like the hardest thing she'd ever had to do. 'I can't believe we just did that.'

'We didn't do anything.' His smile bordered on the regretful and he raked long fingers through his dark hair. 'Unfortunately.'

'How can you say that?' She was pink with embarrassment, her eyes on the door. What if someone had come in? What if someone had caught them? 'We were kissing! In the middle of Resus! In broad daylight!'

He gave her a sexy grin. 'I can switch the lights off if it would make you feel more comfortable.'

She glared at him, her equilibrium disturbed by his smile and his nearness. 'That's not funny.'

His smile faded slowly and his gaze burned into hers. 'Actually, for once I agree with you. None of this is funny.' His voice was soft and he placed an arm either side of her, preventing her escape. 'I can't sleep at night and my concentration is failing. So what are we going to do about it, Dr O'Brien?' His voice was still husky with passion and she felt her body respond instantly.

'Nothing.' There was panic in her tone. 'Absolutely nothing.' Her fingers fumbled and shook as she straightened her clothes. 'We're going to forget this ever happened.' She tried to move away but he didn't budge, his arms like iron bars between her and escape.

'You think that's possible?'

No. 'Yes.' She lifted her chin. *It had to be possible.* 'Of course it's possible. We just have to make an effort and—' She broke off and smoothed her hair, thoroughly flustered. 'We just have to distract ourselves and think about something else.'

'Think about something else.' His gaze dropped to her mouth and lingered. 'Sweetheart, I've been thinking of nothing but you since the day I saw you on the beach dressed in that amazing wetsuit. And then when I saw you in your nightdress…'

His words made her breathing stop and she closed her eyes briefly. 'Josh, *please*. We both know this isn't going to work. We have to be grown-up about it. I'm trying. You have to try, too.'

'Why's that?' His voice was rough and masculine. 'Give me one good reason why.'

Her eyes flew to his. 'You *know* why.' Did he have to look at her like that? It made it almost impossible to breathe, let alone think. 'Because I have Archie.'

He had very dark eyelashes, she noticed absently. And the contrast with the blue of his eyes was amazing.

Those blue eyes lifted back to hers. 'And is Archie enough?'

She swallowed. Up until now, yes. 'I come with a son. I'm not a single woman, Josh.' She said it to remind herself as much as him. 'I have a little boy and he figures in every decision I make. That's the way it has to be and that's the way I want it to be.' She wouldn't have it any other way. She adored her son.

'But surely you're entitled to a part of your life that doesn't include him?' Josh was looking at her now, his blue gaze disturbingly intent. 'Married couples with children aren't just parents, are they? They're still a pair, a couple. They're still allowed a relationship with each other.'

'That's entirely different.'

'Why?'

She swallowed. 'I would have thought that was obvious.' She shrugged awkwardly, wishing he wouldn't stand quite so close. 'If you're parents then you share a commitment so there's no threat to the child's emotional well-being—of course you have a relationship.'

'You sound as though you've swallowed a textbook on child psychology. Theory doesn't always apply to real life, you know.'

She sighed. 'If I have a relationship with a man, Archie could get hurt. I'm not going to let that happen.'

'Does he have to be part of the relationship?' Josh's voice was soft. 'You put him to bed at seven-thirty. What happens after that?'

She stared at him. 'Usually I eat toast and read a textbook.'

He gave a lopsided smile. 'Gripping stuff. I can do a lot better than toast and I'm definitely more interesting than any textbook.'

'I'm sure you are, but—'

'Dinner on Saturday night.' His voice was soft. 'I'll pick you up at eight. That gives you half an hour to get Archie to sleep.'

Her heart pumped against her chest as she faced temptation. 'We're working.'

'Only until seven,' he drawled softly in that deep dark tone that made her knees weak. 'After that we're off until Sunday morning.'

'What exactly are you suggesting?'

He gave a slow smile that was totally male. 'I'm suggesting that we have a nice evening,' he said smoothly, but there was a glint in his eye that took her breath away.

Temptation was dangled in front of her and she felt racked by indecision. For the first time for as long as she could remember, she wanted a man. Really wanted a man. Her body burned in a way she hadn't believed possible. For the first time in ages she was remembering that she was a woman.

Why not?

Why shouldn't she go on a date?

As Josh had rightly said, Archie wouldn't even know about it so it wouldn't cause him a problem. But what about *her?* She bit her lip. Would it cause her a problem?

Where would it all lead?

She looked up at Josh, looked into those wickedly sexy eyes watching her intently. It would lead precisely nowhere, because Josh was a man who liked his bachelor lifestyle.

But at least he was honest about that.

It wasn't as if he was pretending to be something he wasn't. Wasn't as if he was offering something that he couldn't deliver.

'All right.' She didn't know who was more surprised, her or Josh. 'Dinner on Saturday night.' She wouldn't commit to more than that. 'Do you want me to book somewhere?'

He smiled. 'No. Let's do this the old-fashioned way. I want to be the one in control. I'm taking you out, Kat. My choice.'

Her heart flipped and she gave a slight frown. 'We're splitting the bill.'

'Do me a favour.' He placed his fingers over her mouth. 'For one night, leave that fierce independence of yours at home.'

She thought of nothing else for the rest of the week and by Saturday she was so on edge that she could barely concentrate.

It was that kiss, of course, she told herself crossly.

If she hadn't kissed him, she wouldn't have ever known just how well Josh could kiss and she wouldn't now be imagining all sorts of things that she shouldn't be imagining. It was a good thing he couldn't read her thoughts, or she'd be in big trouble.

All week her mind had been somewhere else. She'd been dropping things and staring into space until Hannah had actually asked whether she had a hearing problem.

And all the time Josh had been watching her. Stalking her. His pirate eyes full of promise. Promise of plunder and pillage.

She closed her eyes and tried to talk some sense into herself. Some solid, sensible, single-mother sense. But, no matter how hard she tried, her brain and her body just didn't seem to listen.

Her heart was fluttering with excitement and nerves and no matter how many times she told herself that it was just an evening with a colleague, she couldn't stop the feeling of lightness that spread through her body.

Because, of course, it wasn't just an evening with a colleague.

It was a date.

A date with Josh Sullivan. And when did she ever date? It just wasn't something she did. And she wasn't just worried about the end of the date, and what happened then, she was worried about the date itself.

What if she did something wrong? Or said something wrong? She was out of practice making small talk with men and she wasn't at all sure that she knew the rules. Was she supposed to flirt? Were there certain subjects it was better to avoid?

Cursing herself for behaving like a teenager, she tried to concentrate on the steady stream of minor injuries that flowed through the department on a typical Saturday.

One man had spent too long in the hot August sun and came in looking more than a little embarrassed, his face blistered and red.

'Ouch,' Kat said gently, as she picked up his notes and gestured to the vacant chair. 'Have a seat, Mr Banks. No need to ask what the problem is.' She eyed his scarlet skin with a sympathetic look in her eyes. 'That looks painful. Did you fall asleep in the sun?'

He looked sheepish. 'How did you guess?'

'Because I've seen it before. People always underestimate how hot the sun can be, especially right on the beach because there's so often a breeze. It masks the temperature.' She stood up and washed her hands and then examined his face carefully. 'We usually leave a simple sunburn exposed because it's pretty awkward to get a dressing to stay on the face. Come round to the dressing clinic with me and we'll get it cleaned up.'

She found Hannah finishing off a bandage on a lady with a sprained ankle. 'When you've finished there, could you sort out Mr Banks for me, please?' Kat put his notes in Hannah's tray. 'Just clean it up with diluted chlorohex-

idine solution and then cover it with liquid par-
affin.' She turned to the patient. 'We'll give
you a tube to take home and you need to clean
it twice daily.'

'Can I shave?'

'It's important that you do,' Kat told him as
she wrote instructions in his notes. 'It reduces
the risk of infection. And make sure you sleep
propped up on a couple of pillows for the first
couple of days to reduce the swelling. How
long are you here on holiday?'

'Until the end of the week.'

'Well, it probably goes without saying that
you should stay out of the sun, and if you have
any problems come back to us.' Kat smiled at
him and slipped the pen back in her pocket.
'Enjoy the rest of your holiday.'

She left the patient with Hannah and returned to the cubicle where she was seeing patients. Josh was sprawled in the chair, waiting
for her.

'About tonight...'

Instinctively Kat glanced behind her to
check that no one was listening, and he gave
an amused smile.

'Ashamed of me, Kat?'

Hardly. 'I just don't want to be the subject of gossip.' She was having enough trouble handling her feelings when they were private. She certainly didn't want everyone else to know.

'Neither do I.' He rose to his feet in a smooth movement. 'Do you like Italian?'

At the moment she didn't feel as though she'd be able to eat a thing. Her insides were just too jumbled. But she managed a smile. 'Love it.'

'Good.' He stepped closer. 'Three hours to go.' His voice was low. 'I'll pick you up at the cottage at eight. Can I ring the doorbell, or will that wake Archie?'

She ran her tongue over her dry lips. 'Archie's spending the weekend with Mary because I'm working.'

A slow smile spread across his face. 'So you don't have a curfew?'

'I don't want to be too late.' She felt her cheeks heat. 'I have to pick up Archie the next morning and then we're working.'

'Ah, yes.' He smiled. 'You're a doctor, too, and I'm in your light.'

She blushed as he reminded her of the words she'd used the first time they'd met. 'I thought you were arrogant.'

'I am arrogant.'

No. He wasn't arrogant, and she knew that now. He was incredibly clever and talented. And staggeringly good-looking. But she had no intention of telling him any of those things.

'I'll see you at eight, Dr Sullivan.' And, reaching past him, she picked up the next set of notes.

CHAPTER SEVEN

THE green or the blue?

Kat held both dresses up against her and still couldn't decide.

The green looked good with her hair but it was cut a bit on the low side. The blue was slightly more demure on top but it was far too short. She'd bought it in a sale and then never worn it. In fact, she'd never worn either dress because she didn't go anywhere that demanded that she dress up.

She squinted at herself in the mirror.

They would be sitting down for most of the evening, she reasoned, dropping the green one back on the bed. The blue would be safer.

The silky fabric whispered over her hips and she looked at herself doubtfully. It was like staring at a stranger. This wasn't the person she was, she thought as she turned left and right and studied her svelte outline in the mirror. She was used to dressing like a mother and

204

this dress—she looked at herself long and hard—was designed to make a woman look like a woman.

And just for tonight that was exactly what she was, she reminded herself as she twisted her hair on top of her head and fastened it in place. Tomorrow it would be back to trainers and shorts, but for tonight she was allowed to assume that she wouldn't be chasing a football on a beach or playing six-year-old games.

With that in mind, she left her legs bare, slipping her feet into a pair of strappy sandals that she'd never worn because the heels were too high and impractical for the life she led.

Relieved that Archie was staying with Mary so that she didn't have to proffer explanations for the way she was dressed, she walked into the kitchen and glanced across at Josh's house. He was late. She'd managed to get away but he'd been tied up in Resus. Was he still at work? Or had he changed his mind? The sound of the doorbell made her jump and she resisted the temptation to sprint to the door and yank it open. *Play it cool, Kat,* she told herself firmly, reaching for her bag and taking a deep breath before finally strolling to the front door. This was a one-off. Just one evening of fun between two adults.

She wasn't going to get involved.

She wasn't going to wish for things she couldn't have.

She was just going to have a nice evening, no more than that. For once she was playing woman rather than mother.

Her heart rate increased and her fingers slipped as she fumbled with the lock and opened the door.

And all her resolutions dissolved in an instant.

If ever a man was designed to make a woman forget resolutions, that man was Josh.

'Sorry I'm a bit late. I only escaped from the hospital about twenty minutes ago. Thank goodness for fast sports cars.' His glossy dark hair was still damp from the shower and he had that lazy, sexy look in his eyes that almost made her forget the mechanism of breathing. His gaze slid down her body and he sighed. 'All right—we're going to eat dinner standing up.'

She locked the door of the cottage and dropped the key in her bag. 'Why standing up?'

'Because that way I get to look at your legs all evening.' His eyes were still fixed on her legs. 'That dress is fantastic, although it could have done with being a little shorter.'

'Any shorter and it would be a T-shirt,' she muttered, and he flashed her a grin that was wickedly male.

'Precisely.' He rubbed a hand over the back of his neck and breathed out sharply. 'Is it hot tonight...' his eyes gleamed '...or is it me?'

'It's you.'

'No.' He shook his head, his eyes still on her legs. 'You look amazing. I always seem to be saying that to you. I thought the nightdress was good but this...'

Feeling completely flustered and wishing she'd worn the other dress, she glared at him. 'Can you do me a favour? Can you forget about the nightdress incident?'

He pulled a face and finally looked up from his thorough contemplation of her legs. 'Not sure that I can, to be honest.' His eyes were laughing. 'The memory keeps me awake at night. I'm having evil thoughts.'

She shot him a look designed to wither and followed him down the path to the road, walking carefully. 'You need to think about something else. Oh, Josh!' She stopped dead, totally distracted as she saw the car parked by her cottage. It was a dark, shimmering blue sports car, long and low and completely decadent. She gave a little purr of appreciation deep in her throat. 'It's fantastic.' Reluctantly dragging her gaze away from the car, she turned to him, her gaze mocking. 'Trust you to have a car like this. Does it help you pull women?'

'You think I need help?' The look he gave her would have melted steel and she felt her insides jump and her stomach curl.

No. He didn't need any help at all. 'If you have any success at all in that direction, I'm sure it's because of the car.' Her tone was cool and he threw his head back and laughed.

'You really know how to cut a man down to size. And you still haven't told me what to do about my evil thoughts.'

She was still admiring the car. 'You need to think about something else instead.'

'I've tried that.' He opened the door of the car for her and she slid inside, unable to hold back a little moan of delight as her thighs made contact with the softest leather. For a brief moment she closed her eyes and breathed in, just enjoying the sensation of being in such a fabulous car. Then she felt his breath on her cheek as he leaned forward.

'I've tried thinking about other things.' His voice was low and seductive. 'I've tried thinking about what would have happened that day if you'd been sleeping naked.'

Her eyes flew open and she stopped admiring his car. 'Josh!'

Without warning he dropped a brief, tantalising kiss on her mouth and then strolled around the car and slid into the driver's seat.

For a moment she couldn't move, shocked by the sensation that exploded through her body. Her tongue flickered out and touched her lower lip and she almost groaned aloud at the tantalising reminder of the way he'd touched her.

What happened to her body when he touched her was nothing short of scary. She was a doctor. She was supposed to know all about these things. But there was nothing in the textbooks about the way she was feeling now.

Her whole body was burning up and she felt her legs tremble as he stretched out a hand and turned the key in the ignition. The engine gave a throaty roar and he turned and gave her a slow smile. 'Would you still have come running into my garden if you'd been naked, Kat?'

The chemistry between them was so powerful that she felt as though she was suffocating.

'No!' Her face felt hot. In fact, her whole body felt hot and she wriggled slightly in her seat. 'No, I would not. And the nightdress is hardly indecent. It goes all the way to the floor.'

'And I could see all the way to France through the material,' he said softly, leaning forward and reaching into the glove compartment for his sunglasses. 'And the view was amazing.' His gaze slid to her legs again. 'As it is now. That is a fantastic dress and I love the fact they were short of material when they made it.'

Her cheeks flaming, she tugged at the hemline but the dress wasn't designed for trips in sports cars. Her legs were on display to mid-thigh.

She should have worn the green.

Her hands still on the dress, she glared at him. 'You could look the other way.'

'I could, that's true.' His grin widened and he gave a boyish shrug as he slipped on the shades, obscuring his expression. 'But why would I want to do a thing like that?'

'Because it would be the gentlemanly thing to do?'

'Ah...' He gave her a sexy lopsided smile that was enough to make her forget her own name. 'But I'm not a gentleman. Do you want me to put the top up?'

He wore a linen shirt, open at the throat to reveal a hint of bronzed skin, and she found herself staring and staring.

'Kat?'

'Sorry?' Flustered by the way he was looking at her and feeling thoroughly out of her depth, she looked at him blankly. 'What did you say?'

'The car,' he said patiently. 'It's a sunny evening but we've got a bit of a drive ahead of us and having the top down will mess up your hair.'

She frowned. 'I don't care about my hair. What's the point of driving this fabulous car if you don't have the top down?'

He stared at her for a long moment and then cleared his throat. 'My sentiments exactly.'

'So why ask?'

'It's just that women usually worry about their hair.' He seemed to shake himself. 'Obviously you're not one of them. Right. Let's go, then.'

He drove along the coast road, taking the corners like a racing driver, his large hands firm on the wheel, his movements brief and economical as he got the most out of the road and the car.

And she loved it. Loved the adrenaline rush that came from the speed and the sheer power of the engine, loved the whip of the wind as it tried to grab her hair.

With a laugh of sheer enjoyment, she released her hair from the clasp and let it blow around her head. She forgot to be self-conscious about the length of her skirt. She forgot that she was a single mother with responsibilities. All she thought about was the sheer pleasure of the moment. The wind, the sun, the sea and the spectacular man sitting next to her.

The road hugged the coastline and she saw the sun go down over the sea, watched the tiny yachts bobbing back into the safety of the harbour. Happiness sparkled though her veins like champagne and she couldn't hold back her smile.

It was so beautiful.

Finally he took a tiny, winding road that dropped down to a little fishing village.

'Oh...' She stared at the natural harbour in fascination. 'It's gorgeous. I haven't had time to explore the coast yet.'

'Best fish restaurant in the area.' Josh reversed the car into a space and turned to look at her. 'I prefer your hair like that, by the way. Leave it down.'

Her hair! She'd completely forgotten what the journey must have done to it!

With a gasp she pulled down the vanity mirror and checked her reflection. Her hair fell in a soft, tangled mass around her shoulders. 'Oops.' She gave him a sheepish grin. 'Maybe next time we'd better have the top up.'

And then she remembered that this was just a one-off and that this wasn't a proper date, and she almost squirmed with embarrassment in case he thought she was expecting something more.

She tidied her hair with her fingers and then gave a mental shrug. He obviously didn't mind that it looked messy. Why should she?

He looked at her feet. 'How far can you walk in those?'

'I have no idea.' She spoke without thinking. 'I've never worn them before.'

'You bought new shoes for our date?'

'No!' She grabbed her bag from the car, cross with herself for revealing the fact that she hadn't worn the shoes before. 'I bought them ages ago because I liked them, but then I never actually wore them anywhere because they were so impractical.'

He removed his sunglasses and his eyes glimmered with humour. 'So this is the first impractical date you've had since you bought the shoes?'

It was the first date of any kind. 'Something like that.'

She found it very hard to look away from that smile as she followed him into the restaurant and then out again onto a tiny terrace that overlooked the harbour.

'How did you ever find this place?' Her eyes scanned the pretty yachts and the piles of empty lobster pots. The evening sun branded the sea with fiery streaks of red and gold and the air smelt of the sea and sizzling garlic.

With an appreciative sniff, Kat turned her head towards the kitchen. 'Something smells good.'

'The food here is incredible. Sit down and I'll order some drinks.'

A man emerged from the kitchen and a smile spread across his face. 'Sullivan!' He strode towards them and shook Josh's hand. 'How the devil are you?'

'Good, thanks.' Josh turned to Kat and introduced her. 'This is Mark. He considers himself to be a chef.'

The man grinned and shook her hand. 'Only from Josh would I allow that insult. I almost amputated my finger one night when I was working in the restaurant. Fortunately Josh was here and sorted me out. I've been feeding him ever since.'

Kat smiled. 'Sounds like a good deal.'

'I've saved you our best table, of course.' Mark gestured to a waiter who was hovering with menus. 'They don't need those.' He tucked the menus under his arm. 'You're going to have the scallops followed by the sea bream and then the chocolate *crème brûlée.*'

'Mmm.' Kat's mouth watered and Josh glanced at her, a question in his eyes.

'Sound all right to you?'

'Are you kidding? You're talking to a girl who only had a glass of water for lunch.'

He laughed. 'That's right, so you did. In that case, you should be grateful for anything.' He nodded to Mark. 'Bring it on.'

The waiter delivered a selection of delicious breads to their table and a bowl of shiny olives.

Kat helped herself to an olive and then slipped her hand into her bag and retrieved her mobile phone. 'I just need to be able to hear it,' she muttered by way of explanation, 'in case there's a problem.'

Josh lounged in his chair, watching her. 'Is there usually a problem?'

'I just don't like leaving him.'

'You leave him when you're working.'

'That's different.' She lifted her glass. 'Working is different.'

'So you're not allowed a social life?'

She sipped her wine slowly and then put the glass down on the table. 'Guilt is part of being a single parent.' She shrugged. 'I have to work. It's a fact of life and I don't have any choice about that. But the rest of the time I want to be with Archie.'

Except for tonight, when she didn't want to be anywhere except exactly where she was.

'You say you have to work.' He passed her some bread. 'Doesn't his father give you any financial support?'

Kat shook her head. 'When he found out I was pregnant, he ran so fast he left skid marks.'

Josh looked shocked. 'He's never seen Archie?'

'No.' Kat sat back as the waiter delivered their starters. She stared at the plate in admiration. 'Wow. That's almost too pretty to eat.'

'Almost, but not completely.' Josh picked up his knife and fork, his eyes still fixed on her face. 'I can't believe he just abandoned you.'

Kat shrugged. 'He's a man, and plenty of men are programmed to avoid fatherhood at all costs. Unfortunately I picked one of them.'

'But who looked after you when he was born? How did you manage?'

'I looked after myself. And I looked after Archie. And I managed because I had no choice. I'm not helpless, Josh.' She picked up her fork. 'I do perfectly well on my own.'

She'd been doing it for years and she was used to living that way. She didn't depend on anyone for anything.

'By making sacrifices that no woman should have to make and by working so hard that you have black rings under your eyes.' He looked at her. 'Don't think I haven't noticed.'

Should she tell him that he was the cause of the black rings?

That since he'd kissed her she hadn't been able to sleep?

'I'm just a bit tired.'

'What about your parents? Didn't they give you any support?'

'They weren't exactly pleased when they discovered I was pregnant.' She stared at her plate. 'For six years it's pretty much been me and Archie against the world.'

'I'm beginning to understand why you're so fiercely independent. What about men?'

'No time and no inclination. And not a lot of confidence in my own judgement. Clearly I'm a lousy judge of men.' She kept her tone light and took a mouthful of her starter. 'I don't date. It's easier that way for everyone concerned.'

The sun dipped behind the headland and the candle in the centre of the table danced in the evening breeze. And from across the table Josh watched her, his eyes glittering in the semi-darkness. 'If you don't date…' His voice was a soft, male drawl. 'What are you doing here with me, Kat?'

She'd been asking herself the same question. And she looked around now and asked herself the question again. She looked at the pretty candles on the tables. The expensive wine. The couple next to them enjoying a romantic evening. She looked at the harbour and the stars in the sky and the handsome, sexy man sitting across from her. The evening couldn't have been more perfect.

But this wasn't her life. It didn't feel like her life.

What was she doing, sitting on this pretty terrace, sipping wine with a man who drew every female eye in the room?

Dreaming?

Indulging a feminine fantasy?

Aware that he was waiting for an answer, she managed a smile that said nothing. Revealed nothing. 'Eating a delicious meal, enjoying a fabulous view and drinking the best sauvignon blanc I've ever tasted?'

He laughed. 'That's it?'

'What else is there?' This time her smile was teasing. 'Are you looking for flattery? Do you want me to tell you that you look hot, Dr Sullivan?'

'Do I look hot, Dr O'Brien?'

Something shifted and curled deep in her pelvis. Something dangerous. *Oh, yes, he looked hot.*

'Come on, Josh.' She kept her tone light and avoided his question. 'We both know the sort of man you are. You live for the moment. So let's enjoy the moment and stop worrying about tomorrow. Tell me about you. I already know about the fast car. Now tell me about that boat in your garden.'

He smiled and leaned back in his chair. 'I have two boats. The one in my garden I'm restoring.' His fingers closed round his glass.

'Just a hobby, but it's as good a way as any to spend a day off when I'm not on the water.'

Kat finished her starter. 'And the other boat?'

'The other boat I race.' He fingered his glass, a strange light in his eyes as he looked at her. 'And she's as fast as the wind.'

She saw the glitter in his eyes, the wicked tilt of his mouth as he smiled, and her breath caught in her throat.

Pirate.

'Who do you sail with?'

'Mac, a couple of GPs from the village…' He lifted his glass and drank. 'There's no shortage of crew in a place like this.'

Kat listened, enjoying adult company for the first time in ages. She couldn't remember the last time she'd sat with a man like this and talked. Really talked. And Josh was good company. He had a sharp brain and an equally sharp sense of humour. She found herself telling him about her childhood in Ireland, growing up next to the beach and how she'd dreamed of the same for Archie. She found herself telling him about her plans for the cottage. In fact, she found herself telling him things she hadn't shared with another living soul.

And it felt good. Just this once, it felt good.

Josh settled the bill, ignoring Kat's protest that she should pay half.

'Fancy a walk before we set off?'

'In these shoes?'

He looked down at her feet. He'd forgotten about the shoes. 'Why do women choose shoes like that?'

'Because they're pretty and frivolous and it's fun to keep looking at your feet?'

He laughed. 'I'll remember that next time I'm shopping for shoes.' It was probably safer not to point out that it wasn't her feet he was looking at. That it was her amazing, endless legs that held his attention in that equally amazing short dress. He took her hand and they walked back to the car. 'We'll drive back a different way. There's something I want to show you.'

The shoes added a good three inches to her height and suddenly the top of her head was almost level with his chin. Her scent wrapped itself around him, teasing and seductive. Was it her perfume or her shampoo? He wasn't even sure. He just knew that it oozed into his senses and fed his frustration.

He unlocked the car and held the passenger door open while she slid inside.

'Where are we going?

'It's a secret.' He started the engine and looked over his shoulder as he reversed the car out of the space.

'You mean you haven't decided.'

'Oh, I've decided.' Pressing on the accelerator, he watched her lips part in a soft gasp and decided that she looked good in his car. Her hair shimmered over her shoulders in the semi-darkness and her eyes shone green with delight.

'I love this car.'

He changed gear and the car gave a throaty roar and shot up the hill towards the coast road. 'I want to show you my favourite place.'

He drove for five minutes and then pulled off the road into a field.

'You can't park here!'

'Watch me.' He released both seat belts, reached for a torch from the glove compartment and then sprang out of the car. 'Come with me.'

She let him take her hand. 'Where are we going?'

'You'll see in a minute.' He led her onto the soft grass and then paused. 'You could take your shoes off here, if you like. The ground is soft.'

She did as he'd suggested, her hair flowing forward over her face as she bent down to slip off her shoes. 'If I tread in a cow pat, your car will suffer.'

'No cows.' Without the shoes the top of her head reached his shoulder and he felt suddenly protective. She was almost impossibly slender. 'Come on.'

Despite the darkness he walked confidently, occasionally flashing the torch to check where they were going. After a few minutes he turned sharp right and started walking down towards the sea.

She tugged at his hand, nervous in the semi-darkness. 'We're going to fall off the edge of the cliff!'

'Don't be ridiculous.' He dragged her against him. 'We're almost there.'

They dropped down a bit further and he heard her gasp. 'Oh, Josh, it's amazing.'

The night was clear enough for her to see the rocks and the abandoned lighthouse that stood proudly on the headland.

'We call it Smugglers' Cove.' He tightened his grip on her hand and led her down the grass. 'Most of the tourists don't even know it's here because you can't see it from the road and there's no car park.'

'So whose field did you park in?'

Josh smiled at her. 'He's a farmer. He had a nasty accident on his tractor a few years ago and I patched him up. He doesn't mind if I use his field.'

'Have you patched everyone up?'

'It sometimes feels like it. There.' He stopped and pulled her against his side. 'Legend has it that if you stand here when there's a full moon you can hear the sound of ship-wrecked sailors crying out for help.'

'Cheerful.' But she fell silent and listened to the sound of the waves crashing against the rocks and the soft sigh of the water as it swirled over the sand and retreated. 'Are there any wrecks along this coast?' Her voice was a hushed whisper and she pressed closer against him.

'Several.' He could feel the warmth of her body pressing against his and he felt her shiver. 'Are you scared?'

He felt her hesitation and then she turned to him. 'Not scared.' And then she lifted her face to his and her eyes glittered green in the moon-light. 'Not scared.'

Their eyes held for a long moment and then his self-control snapped and he brought his mouth down on hers with savage urgency.

With a moan of relief and a greed that matched his own, she dropped her shoes, hooked her arms around his neck and kissed him back.

And it was a kiss like no other. As wild as the sea that licked the coast behind them and as bright as the moon that shone above them, it went on and on as they explored, tasted and teased each other to distraction.

He slid his hands down her back, down the soft fabric of her dress, until his fingers found the soft, silken flesh of her legs. Hot, molten lust flashed through him and he tumbled her gently onto the grass and came down on top of her, careful not to hurt her.

He felt her gasp of need against his mouth, felt her squirm under him, and he slid his hand round her back until he found the zip of her dress and jerked it down. As he ripped the dress from her trembling, heated body, his hands shook and his eyes were dark with need. He couldn't ever remember feeling desperation like this before. It galloped through him, violent and greedy, driving every stroke of his hands and every flick of his tongue.

'Josh…' The sound of his name on her lips penetrated the red haze that surrounded his brain and he lifted his head, his breathing unsteady.

'I need you, Kat.' His voice was rough and he felt her hands jerk at his shirt and fumble with his trousers.

'Yes.' Her voice was a soft gasp in the night air. *'Oh, yes…'*

With a violence he hadn't known he was capable of, he kissed her neck and then slid lower, groaning as he took the tip of one breast into his mouth and discovered the true meaning of pleasure. He felt her nipple harden in instant response, and slid his hand down her body, to the junction of her thighs. Tiny panties were the only clothing that remained on her body and they were damp as his fingers probed and then slipped inside her.

His hottest fantasies became reality and she arched against him, sobbed his name and squirmed under his deliberate caress.

His vision blurred and the need threatened to choke him. He hadn't planned it to happen this way. Not here. Not now. But her hands were stroking him and her soft, sweet body was urging him closer and closer.

With a rough curse he ripped her panties and came down over her, claiming her mouth just a fraction of a second before he claimed her body with his, thrusting deep, his fingers biting hard into her bottom as he held her firm.

He heard her cry out as he filled her, felt her close round him, hot and tight, but he couldn't hold back, couldn't do anything except take her hard and fast, with the sounds of the sea roaring behind him and the cool night air sliding over his heated skin.

She came almost instantly and he felt her body pulse around him, driving him closer and closer to his own pleasure. Desperately he searched for control but he couldn't find it and he felt his vision blur as he exploded inside her, driving into her with a rhythmic force that sent her tumbling over the edge again with a series of sobbing cries.

Drained and in a state of disbelief, Josh dropped his head onto her bare shoulder and struggled for breath. It took several minutes before he could speak. Several minutes before he could say any of the things he wanted to say.

Finally he lifted his head and looked at her.

Her eyes were closed, her cheeks slightly flushed in the moonlight, and he dropped a gentle kiss on the corner of her mouth.

'Kat, I'm sorry.' His voice was hoarse and tinged with concern. 'I didn't mean it to be like that.'

There was a brief silence and then her soft mouth, bruised from the roughness of his kisses, curved into a soft smile. 'How did you mean it to be?'

He stared down at her, relief flowing through him as he saw the smile. 'Slow. Gentle. Not here. Not in a field with both of us too desperate to even undress. Did I hurt you?'

'No.' Her eyes opened and she looked at him. 'Don't apologise for wanting me so badly you couldn't wait, Josh.' Her voice was husky. 'It wasn't exactly conventional, but I think you just paid me a compliment.'

He groaned and rolled onto his back, taking her with him. 'I don't know what happened—'

He'd never lost control with a woman before and he felt more than a little shocked by his own behaviour.

'Then that's another compliment.'

They lay together, staring up at the stars, and Josh tried to remember a single moment in his life that had felt as perfect as this one. He failed.

She sighed and then sat up and reached for her dress. 'I don't suppose I'll be wearing this again.'

He winced guiltily at the reminder of just how rough he'd been with her. 'I'll buy you a new one. A shorter one.'

She was *so* beautiful, her skin creamy white in the moonlight, her waist narrow and her breasts full. Despite what had happened moments before, he felt himself harden in immediate response.

'Kat?'

Something of his reaction must have been in his voice because she held the dress against her and her swift glance was suddenly shy. 'What?'

'Let's go home so that I can show you what I had planned.' He found that he was holding his breath. He'd never invited a woman back to his house before. He preferred to be the one in control, the one who decided when the evening ended, but somehow, with Kat, everything felt different. He wanted her in his home, *in his bed.* Would she say no? 'Let's go home so that next time I can take more time.'

There was a long silence and then she gave a slow smile and bent to kiss him. 'That sounds good.' Her voice was pure seduction. 'But you're going to have to lend me your shirt to walk back to the car.'

The way she was looking at him, he wasn't at all sure he'd ever be able to walk again, but he certainly intended to give it a try.

And he was prepared to sacrifice every scrap of clothing if that was what it took to persuade her to come home with him.

He reached for his shirt and gently wrapped it around her. 'Let's move.'

CHAPTER EIGHT

SHE knew exactly when Josh fell asleep.

Felt his strong body relax in her arms, heard his breathing steady and she lay still, savouring the sheer perfection of the moment.

After their wild, passionate encounter on the cliff, he'd carried her back to the car and then driven back home with one hand on the wheel and one hand on her leg, the frequent glances he cast in her direction assuring her that he felt the same need and urgency as she did.

And the moment he'd opened the door to his house, he'd shown her just what he'd felt. With his hands and his mouth, he'd driven her to heights that she hadn't known existed and he'd made love to her again and again until she'd thought she'd just die from the pleasure.

It had to end, of course.

No night, however perfect, could last for ever and she stared out of the tall windows of his bedroom, which overlooked the beach, and saw the sun rising. Kat wanted to reach out and stop it, she wanted to cry out and beg for just one more hour of night before daylight came, because somewhere during the evening, or maybe even before, she'd fallen in love with Josh Sullivan.

But the passage of time cut through pleasure like the blade of a knife and the sun mocked her as it rose and threw light into the early morning.

The night was over.

It was time for her to leave.

And she knew it was up to her. She needed to take control and walk away, while her pride was still intact. She'd gone into his arms thinking of nothing but lust but she was leaving them thinking of nothing but love, and those weren't thoughts she could risk sharing with him.

Josh Sullivan didn't fall in love. He didn't want commitment.

And she couldn't afford to give more of herself than she already had. As it was, she couldn't imagine going back to her life, the way it had been only yesterday.

Before Josh.

She couldn't imagine never having this again, never again sharing this level of intimacy with a man.

Safe in the knowledge that he slept, she allowed her fingers to trace the strong muscle of his shoulder, to drift downwards and brush the dark hairs that dusted his chest.

Every part of her ached. Her senses, her body, but most of all her heart.

It was definitely time to leave.

Josh woke to find the bed empty.

He lay still for a moment, registering the strength of the sunlight blazing through the window, registering the silence. There was no clatter of coffee-cups. No sizzle of bacon frying. The emptiness closed around him.

Kat was gone.

With a soft curse he swung his legs out of bed and padded over to the window that faced her cottage, but there was no sign of her.

He glanced at the pile of clothes next to his bed.

There was no sign of her torn, blue dress and there was no sign of his shirt.

He raked long fingers through his roughened dark hair and swore fluently. He remembered the soft little cries she'd made as he'd explored every inch of her. He remembered the way she'd slid her hands over his back and urged him on, urged him to go faster, *harder,* and he let out a sharp breath and ran a hand over his face.

How could she just leave after last night? Hadn't it meant anything to her?

Of course it had meant something to her.

He knew it had.

So why had she left?

Frustrated for the first time in his thirty-two years, he paced barefoot into his kitchen and found some coffee. The irony of the situation didn't escape him. All those occasions he'd avoided bringing women back to his house because he'd been afraid he wouldn't be able to get rid of them, and here he was wishing Kat had left her toothbrush with his.

He ran hand over his face and wondered what was happening to him.

It was just sex, he told himself firmly, pouring coffee into a mug and prowling over to the window again.

Incredible sex, but just sex.

And he was just being contrary. If she'd been lying in the bed when he'd woken up, he would have wanted her to leave. He would have been cursing himself for being so foolish as to bring her to his home. The only reason he was missing her was because *she'd* been the one to walk away.

He gave a half-smile and took a mouthful of coffee.

It was typical of Kat to want to be the one in control.

Typical of her to show him that it was just the one night.

And typical of her to be different to every other woman he'd ever met.

But he wasn't prepared to settle for one night. He drained his coffee, feeling the kick of caffeine stir his brain.

And if she truly thought it was ending after one night, she knew nothing about him.

*   *   *

Kat arrived at work the next day wishing there was some way she could avoid Josh.

She wasn't at all sure she could work alongside him and not betray her true feelings.

How could she ever have thought that a night with Josh would be just a one-off? That she'd be able to walk away without a second thought?

She must be have been delusional.

She felt confused and nervous and vulnerable, but most of all she was angry with herself. Angry with herself for giving in to temptation. But give in she had, and now she was paying the price. She'd unlocked a part of herself that she'd kept hidden securely away, and now she was going to struggle to return to the way life had been before.

In the staffroom, she changed into her scrub suit and lingered for a moment before finally plucking up the courage to walk onto the unit.

She'd got herself into this situation, she reminded herself crossly, looping her stethoscope around her neck, and she just had to deal with it. All she had to do was concentrate on the patients. She wasn't going to think about an abandoned lighthouse or the way the soft grass had felt against her bare skin. *And she wasn't going to think about his hands and mouth moving over her body.*

'Dr O'Brien, I presume.' Josh's soft drawl came from directly behind her and she gave a gasp and turned to find him leaning against the wall, watching her.

His blue gaze was disturbingly intent. 'I thought it was Archie that did the magic in the family.'

Just seeing him again made her body heat. He looked tough and male and more attractive than any man had a right to be. 'I don't know what you mean.'

'I'm talking about your disappearing act,' he drawled, his eyes dropping to her mouth. 'One moment you were in my arms. The next minute you were gone. Clearly my technique needs work.'

She gave a gasp of shock. 'Josh, this is hardly the place—'

'It's a perfectly good place.' He grabbed her arm and pulled her against him, and she felt the heat of his body burn through the thin fabric of her scrub suit. 'You just walked out on me without so much as a goodbye.'

She tried to free herself but his arm slid round her waist. 'Well, goodbye didn't seem the right thing to say.'

'So instead you chose to say nothing.' He glared down at her, streaks of colour lighting his cheekbones. 'For crying out loud, Kat, we made love all night! You fell asleep in my arms! And then you walked out as if we were strangers.'

'Keep your voice down!' Her face turned scarlet and she glanced around self-consciously, but fortunately there was no one else in the corridor. 'What's the matter with you, Josh? You said yourself that you'd never invited a woman back to your house before. You know as well as I do that this was just a one-night stand.'

'I never said anything about it being a one-night stand.' He frowned. 'I don't have one-night stands. What sort of a man do you think I am?'

'A single one!' This time she managed to wriggle free and she backed away from him, pushing a strand of hair away from her flushed face. 'You're single, Josh! And I'm not.' Aware that her voice had risen, she took a deep breath and forced herself to speak calmly. 'I have a son and he features in everything I do.'

'He didn't feature last night.'

She closed her eyes. She didn't want to think about last night. 'Last night was a one-off, we both know that.'

'I don't know that.' His jaw was hard and uncompromising and there was a dangerous glint in his eyes.

She sighed. 'You're acting as though we have a relationship, and we both know that's just ridiculous. We don't have a relationship, Josh. It was just sex. That's all it ever was.'

There was a brief silence while he scrutinised every inch of her face. 'What we shared was much more than just sex,' he purred softly, 'and you know it, Kat.'

His tone was lethally smooth and she tugged away from him, desperate to put some distance between them. She couldn't stand the way he was looking at her with those lazy, sexy, blue eyes. As if he wanted to throw her down on the floor and make love to every inch of her. As if this was the beginning of something. *As if they had a future...*

She gave herself a mental shake, infuriated with herself for fantasising again. It was *definitely* time to end the conversation.

'Wait a minute.' He caught her arm again, refusing to let her go. 'Are you really saying that's it? Are you serious? Last night was just a one-off?'

'Of course it was.' She looked at him in exasperation. 'What else could it possibly be? Like I said, I have a child and you're a single guy.' *A sexy, single guy.* 'End of story.'

His eyes were suddenly cold. 'I can't believe you mean that.'

For a moment her heart gave a little leap and then she remembered that this was probably a man thing. They always had to be the one in control.

'Why? Because your ego is dented? Because you weren't the one to finish it. It's hard to finish what we never started.'

'Ouch. I definitely need to work on my technique.' His eyes lifted slowly and burned into hers and frustration and misery exploded inside her.

'This isn't about your technique, Josh!' She virtually shouted the words and then groaned with embarrassment as a passing doctor from another department shot a startled look in their direction. 'Oh, help, now *everyone* will know.'

He didn't flinch. 'And what if they do?'

'I—have—a—child!' she emphasised each word, wondering what it took for him to understand. 'I don't want him thinking that his mother is a—' She broke off and he lifted an eyebrow.

'A what? An attractive, intelligent, moral woman with a right to a grown-up life of her own?'

She closed her eyes. 'It doesn't work that way, Josh. It just isn't that simple.'

'So you won't go out with a man unless there's a proposal of marriage on the table?'

She stared at him blankly. 'Marriage? Is that what you think? That I want marriage?' She shook her head. 'Forget it. A piece of paper doesn't signify commitment. You can relax, Josh. I don't want to marry you.'

If her heart hadn't been in the process of being demolished, she would have laughed at the thought. Marriage? If that was what he thought she wanted, no wonder he looked so tense.

'So what do you want?'

'To go back to the way we were! To be able to sleep at night. I don't know! *I don't know what I want.*' She raked her fingers through her hair, all the frustrations of the last few weeks pouring into her voice. 'To be able to get you out of my mind for two minutes and concentrate on my work would be a good start!'

There was a long, pulsing silence and she bit back a groan as she realised just how much she'd revealed.

'You're not sleeping because you're thinking of me?'

'Josh, please...'

'Is it true?' His voice sounded strange and she looked at him wearily.

'So what if it is? It doesn't change anything.'

'Yes, it does. It means you could be throwing away something that has a future.'

She watched a nurse pass and then turned back to him, her heart thumping against her chest. 'What are you saying?'

He ran a hand over the back of his neck and looked vaguely uncomfortable. It occurred to her that it was the first time she'd ever seen Josh out of his depth. 'I don't know really.' He gave a casual shrug, his gaze slightly wary. 'I suppose I'm saying that if you're awake at night thinking about me and I'm awake at night thinking about you then we may as well give it a go. This whole relationship thing.'

If she hadn't been hurting so badly, she would have laughed at the expression on his face. He looked *so* uncomfortable. As if he wanted to reach out and grab the words and drag them back into his mouth.

But at least he'd said them, and for some reason she felt a lump building in her throat. 'I realise that's a very flattering offer, coming from you.' She managed a smile. 'But it isn't enough, Josh. You don't just try a relationship on for size and see how it works when there's a child involved.'

He sucked in a breath. 'I know you're looking for guarantees, but the truth is those just don't exist for anyone. This is the real world, Kat. All people can do is their best. Who knows what's round the corner? All I know is that you should grab the moment and live.'

Which was what he did, of course. He drove his fast cars, strove to catch the biggest wave on his surfboard and raced his boat. He was a man who lived life to the full, every moment of every day. Whereas she—she swallowed as she scrutinised her own life—tried to make her life as predictable and safe as possible. Tried to control every minute.

'I like my life the way it is.'

'Do you? Do you really? You're missing out, Kat,' he said roughly, 'and what's more, Archie is missing out, too. By trying to protect him from everything, you're robbing him of experiences that might enrich his life. I don't pretend to know anything about parenting, but how's he ever going to learn to cope with problems if you make sure he never has any?'

'As you say, you don't know anything about parenting.' She stepped away, her voice cold.

'And Archie has a very happy life. If I get involved with you and it all goes wrong, as it inevitably will—'

'Why inevitably?' His voice was harsh and she looked at him with exasperation.

'Oh, come on, Josh! We both know children aren't on your agenda.'

'Maybe they are.' His eyes glittered strangely, 'Maybe I've just never really thought about the whole children thing before now.'

She stared at him. 'You're saying you want children?'

'I don't know what the hell I'm saying!' He stabbed his fingers through his hair and let out a long breath. 'I just know that this wasn't a one-night stand for me.'

'Well, I can't expose Archie to hurt while you're making up your mind what you really want,' she snapped, 'so it's obviously best for everyone if we don't get involved.'

He caught her face in his hands and forced her to look at him. 'We're involved, Kat,' he growled, his tone hovering between anger and frustration. 'We're already involved. Think about that next time you're lying awake at night unable to sleep.'

He stared down into her eyes and then, with a soft curse, his hands dropped to his sides and he strode away from her into the department.

The rest of the week was a nightmare.

Kat was exhausted from a combination of lack of sleep and work pressure and her concentration had never been worse. Her head was filled with nothing but Josh and it didn't help that whatever she was doing, wherever she was standing, he was always right there next to her.

What was she going to do? she wondered helplessly a week after their date. How was she ever going to get him out of her mind? Was she going to have to leave Cornwall?

But then she thought of her cottage by the beach and how happy Archie was, and she knew that wasn't an option. She couldn't leave a place that they both loved so much.

And she couldn't leave Josh.

Tears pricked her eyes as she tried to concentrate on the X-ray she was studying. Even though she couldn't be with him in the way she wanted, she knew that she'd rather live with him on the edges of her life than absent from it.

She was just tired, she told herself firmly, yanking the X-ray out of the light-box and returning it to its brown protective cover. Tomorrow was her day off and she was going to catch up on some sleep. Maybe then she'd be more rational.

No matter how hard she tried, she couldn't forget what Josh had said about Archie. Was he right? Was Archie really missing out, too? In trying to protect him, was she depriving her son of experiences that would enrich his life?

She just didn't know. All she knew was that her mind felt tangled and confused and her eyes ached from lack of sleep.

When she eventually finished her shift she virtually dragged herself to Mary's to collect Archie and then drove home.

'In the morning, do you think you could watch children's television until I wake up?' She unlocked the door and let them both into the house. 'Mummy's a bit tired.'

Archie dropped his swimming bag on the floor and frowned at her. 'Are you sad? You look sad.'

He was so observant. 'I'm not sad,' she lied, bending to hug him. 'Just very tired.'

'Maybe we should go round and play with Josh,' Archie suggested cheerfully. 'Josh always makes you smile and you get that funny look on your face when you're with him.' He gave a little shrug and sprinted through to the kitchen.

For a moment Kat just stared and then she followed him. 'What do you mean by that?'

Archie dragged a chair across the room and then climbed up and opened a cupboard. 'You're always smiling when you're with Josh. And so's he.' He stood on tiptoe and reached for a cup. 'You both smile. So maybe tomorrow we could all spend the day together.' The cup clasped in his hand, he jumped down from the chair. 'We could even invite him for a sleepover. That would be fun.'

'A sleepover?' She felt her face heat. Did he know something? She shook herself. Of course he didn't. He was only six years old, for goodness' sake, and he was speaking six-year-old language. 'Why would you invite him for a sleepover?'

'Because that's what you do with friends, and Josh is a friend,' Archie said patiently, his glance telling her that he clearly thought she was a bit stupid. 'Do you think he'd fit in the snuggle sack I had from Father Christmas?'

'I— Well...' Kat raked her fingers through her hair and smiled weakly. 'Probably not, sweetheart. I think he's a bit too big.'

'He could just sleep in the spare bed, then.' Evidently considering the problem solved, Archie moved the chair along, climbed up again and switched on the tap. 'Can we have fish fingers for tea?'

Fish fingers.

The reality of her life.

Kat forced a smile. 'Of course. Fish fingers it is. And in the morning, will you tiptoe downstairs? When I wake up I promise we'll go to the beach and have fun.'

'Can we go and see Josh?'

'No!' There was a note of panic in Kat's voice and instinctively she modulated her tone. 'No, sweetheart. Not tomorrow.'

'But he doesn't mind. He said so.' Archie stepped into his trunks, his eyes huge. 'He promised I could help with the boat and practise my knots.'

'And so you can. Another time.' When she'd managed to put her one incredible night with Josh well and truly behind her. And so far she hadn't done very well. 'Tomorrow it's just us, like it always has been. That's good, isn't it?'

He looked at her and shrugged, disappointment written all over his face. 'I suppose so.'

She felt something tug inside her. *Why did life have to be so complicated?*

CHAPTER NINE

HOPING that physical activity would burn off some of the frustration that had kept him sleepless for yet another long and restless night, Josh rose early and spent the first hour of the day clearing out the shed that he used to store all his sailing gear.

By the time he'd emptied everything out, earmarked a few things for the skip and tidied the rest away, he decided he'd earned breakfast.

For the first time since he'd woken up, he glanced up the path towards Kat's cottage and froze as he saw Archie leaping along the path towards him.

Conscious that he was desperately in need of a shave and a shower, he searched for signs of Kat but the boy was on his own.

Of course he was on his own, Josh thought savagely as he slammed the door of the shed closed and reached for a rag to wipe his hands on. Kat had made it perfectly clear that she didn't want anything to do with him.

He gave a sigh as the boy drew close, his eyes shining with excitement at the prospect of the new day.

Was it really fair to blame Kat for wanting to protect something so precious?

And she was right, wasn't she? He couldn't be trusted with her most valued possession. He didn't have any of the skills necessary to make a good, reliable father. He didn't know anything about what was expected.

Hell, he didn't even know what he wanted out of life any more and she was right when she said that he shouldn't be allowed to experiment with Archie.

'Would you fit into a sleepover sack?' Archie bounded up to him, as eager as a puppy, his clothes on inside out as usual. 'Because Mum reckons you'd be too big.'

'Sorry?' Josh reached for his own shirt, which he'd slung over the bench before he'd started work. He stared at it for a moment then gave a little smile and pulled it inside out.

'I want you to come for a sleepover.' Archie hurried across to the boat and touched the hull carefully. 'But Mum thinks you'd be too big to fit in my sleepover bag.'

Josh dragged the shirt over his head. 'A sleepover?'

Archie gave an impatient sigh. 'You know—you spend the night at our house! It's what friends do. And if you talk in really soft voices you can get to stay up *really* late.' He glanced over his shoulder, checking that no one was listening. 'The trick is to know how to act asleep when Mum puts her head round the door.'

Josh looked at him, intrigued. 'So how do you act asleep?'

'You move a bit,' Archie confided, lowering his voice. 'People who are really asleep don't always lie still. I know that because once I lay like a stone and Mum said, ''I know you're awake, Archie,'' in *that voice* of hers.'

Josh gave a wry smile. He suspected he'd been on the receiving end of 'that voice'.

'Anyway...' Archie gave a little shrug '...I'm going to have Marcus for a sleepover the next time Mum has a day off. But you could come any time. It's not as if Mum has to give you a lift home or anything.'

At a loss for words, Josh ran a hand over his rough jaw and decided that a conversation with a child was every bit as challenging as a conversation with a woman.

'Does your mum want me to come for a sleepover?'

Archie was studying the boat again. 'She doesn't think you'll fit in the bag. Can I help you paint this again?'

'Does your mum even know you're here?'

Archie shook his head and wriggled under the boat. 'She's asleep. I'm supposed to be watching television.'

'Hold it!' Josh raised his hands and took several steps backwards. 'If she doesn't know you're here, then you're going straight home, right now this minute.'

Archie gaped at him. 'You're sending me home?'

'That's right,' Josh said hastily, grabbing his arm and leading him back towards the path. 'The last time you came here without telling her, your mum yelled at me. She used *that voice*. You know the one!'

'So?' Archie rolled his eyes. 'She yells at me all the time, and I'm smaller than you! Are you telling me you're scared of my mum?'

Josh hid the smile. 'Terrified.' Terrified that if he did the wrong thing she wouldn't have any more to do with him. 'And you're going home right now.' He dropped the cloth he'd been using to clean his hands. 'And what's more, I'm taking you myself just to be sure that you don't get into mischief on the way.'

Archie turned his head to look at the cottage then looked back at Josh. 'It's so close you can practically touch it. I can go on my own.'

'I don't care. I'm still walking you back to the door.'

But before Josh could move, a car pulled into his drive and Louisa climbed out.

'Hopeful!' With a shriek of delight Archie dashed over to hug the dog and was soon rolling around on Josh's lawn, in danger of being licked to death.

Josh looked at his sister-in-law and then at the car. 'I can't believe you can still fit into that car—can you even reach the steering-wheel?'

'Don't be rude.' She stood on tiptoe to kiss his cheek. 'I've been baking and I thought you might like some. Then I'm off to the baby shop to pick up a couple of things. Can you unload my boot for me?'

Josh took the keys from her and unlocked the boot, lifting out several bags and a cake tin.

'I wish this backache would go away. I've had it for days.' She rubbed a hand over her back and tilted her head to one side as she watched the dog and the boy playing together. 'What's Archie doing here?'

'Giving me a headache as usual.' Josh slammed the boot shut. 'I'm just taking him back over to Kat. Wait here and then I'll make us some coffee.'

He strode through to put the bags in his kitchen and Louisa followed.

'You know, Josh, you really ought—' She broke off and gasped, her pretty face suddenly contorted in pain. 'Oh, Josh.' She grasped the back of a chair and put a hand on her bump.

'What?' Josh dropped the bags and strode to her side. 'What, Louisa?'

She gave another gasp that turned to a sob. 'I think…' Her breath caught and for a moment she couldn't speak. 'I think the baby is coming.'

'What?' He gaped at her. 'Don't be ridiculous.'

Louisa made a sound somewhere between a laugh and a groan. 'When did you last look at me? I'm nine months pregnant, Josh. It has to come out some time.'

'But not here! Not now!' Josh felt a sudden rush of panic and forced himself to stay calm. He was a doctor, for heaven's sake! 'OK.' He jabbed his fingers through his hair and tried to think straight. 'Well, that's fine. That's good. It's not due for a couple of weeks but this is fine. It's really not a problem. We'll just get you to hospital and I'll give Mac a ring and—'

'Josh.' She grabbed his arm and he winced with pain as her fingers dug hard into his flesh. He'd always thought his sister-in-law was gentle. *Where had she learnt how to grip like that?*

'Josh.' She was gasping now. 'There isn't going to be time to go to hospital.'

He stared at her blankly. 'What do you mean, there isn't going to be time to go to hospital? This is your first baby. First babies take hours—days even.'

They didn't just arrive without warning. *In his kitchen.*

She screwed up her face again and made a sound in between a moan and a giggle. 'You don't know anything about babies, Josh. Some of them come quickly.'

He ran a hand over the back of his neck, feeling the prickle of sweat cool his skin. 'Not the first time. The first time they take ages and—'

'Josh! Shut up, will you?' There was a tinge of panic in her voice and more than a touch of exasperation. 'Stop telling me what it says in the textbooks!' She gritted her teeth and held onto him harder. 'I'm telling you this baby is coming. I can feel it.'

He heard the fear in her tone and instantly snapped into professional mode. He dealt with people's fear on a daily basis. He could deal with fear. It was the baby he wouldn't be any good with.

'All right, let's sit you down.' He pulled out a kitchen chair but she refused to let go of his arm.

'I don't think I want to sit down.' She gave a tiny whimper and rubbed her bump. 'I want to walk, or push.'

Push?

'Don't push!' Josh felt sweat break out on his brow. *This couldn't be happening to him. He should have stayed in bed. He should have—*

'*Josh!*'

'Please, don't push.' He wondered if there was any way he could remove his arm from her grip without offending her. At this rate he was going to need stitches. 'Not until we know what's going on. I'm going to ring Mac and—'

'No!' She still held him tightly. 'Don't leave me. I tell you I'm going to have this baby on your kitchen floor any moment.' She gave a hysterical laugh that turned into a sob and Josh eyed his mobile phone, which was just out of reach. If she'd let go of him for a second, he'd be able to grab it and call someone.

'Louisa—'

'Hopeful wants something to eat.' Archie walked into the kitchen and stopped dead, his eyes popping out of his head. 'What's the matter with Louisa? Her face is all funny.'

Josh gritted his teeth. 'Her baby is coming.' And that probably wasn't something a six-year-old was meant to see. What did six-year-olds know about babies? He didn't want to frighten him.

But Archie looked more excited than frightened. 'Here? Now?'

'Here. Now.' Josh wiped his brow with his forearm and was suddenly struck by inspiration. 'Archie, I need you to do something for me. I need you to pass me my phone from over there and then go to your house and wake your mum up.' Hadn't she told him that her last job had been in obstetrics? 'Tell her that Louisa is having her baby and that she needs to get over here now. Do it, Archie.' He gritted his teeth as Louisa almost amputated his arm with her fingers. 'Do it now!'

Archie looked at him then grabbed the phone, virtually threw it at Josh and then disappeared back through the door at a run.

From the depths of sleep, Kat heard her name and shot out of bed, her heart racing. 'What? Archie? Is that you?'

'You need to come now!' He raced into her bedroom, panting and almost bursting with excitement. 'It's an urgency.'

Urgency? Still half-asleep, she tried to translate. Urgency? Emergency? 'What's an emergency? What are you talking about?'

'The baby's coming and Josh doesn't know anything and you have to *come now!* He said so or it's going to drop on the floor.'

'What baby? What floor?' She grabbed her shorts but Archie pulled at her arm.

'You haven't got time to change. It's coming. It will probably be on the kitchen floor by now. You have to hurry.'

'What will? Who will?' *What was he talking about?* 'What baby?'

He looked at her as though she were stupid. 'Louisa's baby! It's coming out of her tummy and Josh is looking *really* weird. He's got that face I use when you make me eat broccoli! And you need to *come now!*'

'Oh, my God...' Suddenly understanding what he was trying to tell her, Kat slipped her feet into her trainers and raced after him, wondering how he knew that Louisa's baby was coming.

She ran into Josh's house and found him crouched on the floor next to Louisa, who was sobbing and fighting for breath.

'It's OK, sweetheart.' Josh had his arm round Louisa's shoulders and was desperately trying to reassure her, but there was no missing the relief on his face when he saw Kat. 'She thinks she's having the baby.'

'I don't *think,* you great idiot,' Louisa yelled, thumping him hard with both her fists. '*I know.* Do you think I'm *stupid* or something? Do you think I *don't know when I'm having a baby?*'

Josh flinched and Kat tried not to smile. Josh was such a talented doctor that she'd never imagined a situation where he'd be out of his depth, but clearly this was one of them.

'Have you examined her?'

He looked at her in horror. 'She's my sister-in-law,' he muttered, and Kat gave a sigh.

'She's a woman in labour, Josh, and judging from the way she's cursing and thumping you I'd say she was in transition. We need to examine her. She mustn't push before she's fully dilated or she could damage her cervix.'

The look on Josh's face was so comical that Kat couldn't help laughing. 'Calm down, Josh. Childbirth is a normal part of life. It isn't an illness.'

'I think I prefer illness.'

She walked into the room and crouched down next to Louisa, her voice calm. 'Louisa, you're going to be fine, sweetheart. There is absolutely nothing for you to worry about. My guess is you're in transition and this is the worse bit. Just carry on swearing and thumping Josh and in a minute it will pass.'

'But whether I'll be alive at the end of it is another matter entirely,' Josh muttered darkly, wincing as Louisa's fingers dug deeper into his flesh. He eased himself away. 'I'll put the kettle on. Don't you need hot water? In the movies they always have loads of hot water at the ready. I'll get you hot water.'

Kat let out a sigh and wondered what had happened to his usually razor-sharp brain. Then she caught the look in his eyes and realised what was the matter. *He was worried about Louisa.* 'Putting the kettle on sounds like a great idea. Once it's boiled you can make me a nice, strong cup of coffee,' she said calmly, 'because I've just woken up and I need some help. And pretty soon Louisa will want a cup of tea. Do you have any medical equipment at all in this house?'

'I can run to gloves. Nothing else. I called an ambulance. And Mac is on his way.'

'Well, I have a feeling this baby might not be prepared to wait. Get me the gloves, Josh.' They were better than nothing. 'And I need some help to move Louisa to your sofa. She'll be more comfortable there.'

Louisa screwed her face up and held onto Kat's hand. 'All that backache I've been having—I must have been in labour and I never knew.' She gave a tiny mew of panic. 'I'm scared, Kat—I should be in hospital.'

'Nonsense. I can't think of a better place to have a baby than at home with people who love you.' Kat crouched down and took her hand. 'You've just got yourself all in a panic and you've forgotten about your breathing. With the next contraction I want you to breathe with me—remember everything they taught you in those hideously boring classes.' She slid a hand onto the top of Louisa's abdomen and felt it begin to tighten. 'Right, now, breathe— that's it. Good…fabulous.' She coached Louisa through the breathing, waited for the contraction to pass and then gestured for Josh to help her move Louisa onto the sofa.

Then she quickly washed her hands and slipped on the gloves. 'We need to check that your cervix is fully dilated and effaced before you begin pushing, Louisa,' she explained, 'so I'm just going to examine you.'

'I'll go out and check on Archie and see if there are any signs of an ambulance,' Josh muttered, backing away so fast he almost fell over.

Kat was concentrating on Louisa. 'This might be a bit uncomfortable.' She felt what she needed to feel and decided that it was a good thing that her last job had been in obstetrics. 'Well, you're completely right, of course. This baby is coming any minute,' she said calmly, then looked up to see Josh standing there, a strange expression on his handsome face.

'It's coming? Really?'

Kat smiled. 'Yes, it's coming. And everything seems fine. Relax.'

Something flickered in his blue eyes. 'I'm going to be an uncle...' Stunned, he blinked for a few moments and then seemed to suddenly stir himself. 'What do you want me to do?'

Finally he sounded like the Josh she knew and Kat breathed a sigh of relief, knowing that, if things didn't go according to plan, she might well need his help.

'Get some towels or blankets or something because your wooden floor isn't the best landing mat for a baby. And then calm down and enjoy it. It's not every day you see your own niece or nephew born.'

Louisa screwed her face up. 'I want to push.'

'Then push.' Kat slid an arm round her shoulders and encouraged her, but Louisa gave a tiny sob.

'I want Mac. I really want Mac.'

'He's coming, angel,' Josh said quietly, sitting down beside her and taking her in his arms. 'In the meantime, I'm just going to have to be a substitute. A pretty poor one, I know, but I'm the best there is. Go on, amputate my arms if you need to, but when this is over, I'm cutting your nails.'

Louisa buried her head in his shoulder and laughed. 'But you hate babies and everything to do with children.'

'Whoever told you that?' Josh gave a lop-sided smile and stroked her hair awkwardly. 'I'm brilliant with children. Just ask Archie. I've been practising my technique on him. It still needs a bit of refining but I'm improving daily.'

Grateful that he was distracting and calming Louisa, Kat examined her again. 'This baby is nearly born, Louisa,' she said gently. 'You're doing so well. Just one more push.'

Where was Archie?

Suddenly anxious about her son, she glanced over her shoulder. Josh intercepted the look.

'I told him he's on ambulance duty,' he said roughly. 'I've stationed him in the garden with Hopeful, watching the road. Was that the right thing to do? I thought that a practical lesson in human reproduction might not be appropriate at his age.'

'Exactly the right thing to do.' She was immensely touched that, given everything that was happening, he'd still given thought to Archie's feelings. 'Uncle Josh.' She felt Louisa's abdomen tighten under her hand and turned her attention back to her friend.

'This is it, Louisa. I can see the baby's head.' Remembering everything she'd learned from her time on obstetrics, she watched the head emerge and stopped Louisa from pushing. 'Pant, now, that's it.' Kat encouraged her as the baby's head was born and then let out a breath of relief. So far so good. 'Well done.

You're nearly there, Louisa. The shoulders will come with the next contraction.'

She felt a flicker of panic. What if something went wrong now? What equipment did they have? Nothing…

Then she reminded herself that there was no reason why anything should go wrong. Plenty of women had babies with no problems at all. Why shouldn't Louisa be one of them?

Even as she had the thought, Louisa screwed up her face with the contraction, held tightly to Josh and the baby slithered out into Kat's waiting arms and started to bawl loudly.

Josh breathed out heavily and hugged Louisa tightly. 'You clever thing.' He looked at Kat and a big smile spread across his face. 'And you're a clever thing, too, Dr O'Brien.'

She shared his sense of relief that so far everything had gone smoothly. 'You have a little girl,' she said softly, lifting the baby carefully and giving her to Louisa. Then she wrapped mother and baby in blankets and felt some of the tension drain from her.

Which was all wrong, of course, she mused, because there was still the placenta to deliver and she hadn't cut the cord.

At that moment Archie raced into the room, Hopeful at his heels. 'The ambulance is coming. I heard it and—' He broke off and stared at Louisa and then at his mother. 'Is that it?'

'Not "it", sweetheart,' Kat said gently. 'Her. She's a baby girl.'

'Wow.' Archie tiptoed across. 'Can I see?'

Flushed with her success, Louisa smiled at him and pulled the blanket down so that he could take a closer look. 'Of course you can. Isn't she beautiful?'

Knowing that six-year-olds weren't blessed with tact, Kat held her breath, waiting for Archie to make some ingenuous comment about how wrinkled and screwed up the baby was, but instead he stared in wonder.

'That's amazing. Why is she crying? What's the matter with her?' He looked at Josh. 'I don't understand why she's crying. Does she want something?'

'Don't ask me,' Josh drawled, his eyes fixed on his baby niece. 'She may only be small, but she's still a woman and what they want is always a total mystery to the male species. Get used to it, Arch. It's a fact of life.'

Archie gave a nod and they shared a look of masculine understanding. 'Right. Maybe she just wants a cuddle.' He gave the casual shrug of an expert. 'Girls usually like cuddles.'

'Good idea,' Louisa said, holding the baby closer. The newborn immediately stopped crying and Archie beamed.

'I was right! You see? Simple.'

From outside they heard the roar of an engine and the shriek of sirens, and Mac raced into the house moments later with the paramedics on his heels.

'I got your message. Is she OK? Has she had it?' He stopped dead at the sight of his wife in the arms of his brother, a tiny baby cradled in her arms. 'Oh, my God...'

'Yes, to all those questions. I'm an uncle.' Josh kept his arm round Louisa, a smug expression in his eyes, 'and, if I say so myself, I'm pretty good at it. With Archie's help, we've got this whole baby thing sorted.'

'You delivered the baby?' Mac ran a hand over the back of his neck, gratitude in his eyes as he looked at his brother. 'I don't know what to say. I don't know how to thank you. If you hadn't been here for her…'

'It was nothing. Really.' Josh shrugged modestly and Kat and Louisa stared at each other open-mouthed and exchanged a look that said just one thing.

Men.

CHAPTER TEN

'YOU do realise that you're wearing your nightdress again, Dr O'Brien?'

The ambulance had departed, taking Louisa to hospital, and Josh and Kat were finally left alone in the kitchen while Archie played with Hopeful in the garden.

She glanced down at herself with a wry smile. 'You don't think this is suitable attire for delivering babies?'

His gaze slid down her body. 'Looks perfect to me.' His voice was husky and for a moment their eyes clashed.

She was the first to break the contact, reminding herself of all the reasons why she really shouldn't—*couldn't*—be in love with this man.

'Talking of suitable attire.' She kept her tone as casual as possible. 'Do you realise you're wearing your shirt inside out?'

'Of course. Archie wears his inside out.' He poured coffee into two cups and handed her one. 'And he looks pretty cool. I decided to follow the trend.'

'You're basing your fashion decisions on my son's dress sense?'

'Why not?' He sipped his coffee and she laughed.

'It's probably only fair to warn you that he never spends too much time looking at himself in the mirror.'

'I always considered mirrors a complete waste of space.' Josh ran a hand over his face. 'What a morning. What time is it?'

'Ten o'clock?'

'Is that all?' He gaped at her. 'It feels like midnight.'

'Well, you've crammed quite a lot into your morning, Dr Sullivan,' she pointed out, humour in her eyes as she looked at him. 'After all, you did just deliver Louisa's baby, remember?'

He grinned at her tone and slid his hands round the mug. 'Don't mock my contribution.

My arms and shoulders may never recover. I was in as much pain as she was!'

Kat rolled her eyes. 'I don't think so,' she said dryly, 'but you certainly made more fuss. I could hear you whimpering with panic behind me most of the time,' she added, lifting an eyebrow in his direction. 'Babies not your thing, Dr Sullivan?'

His smile faded slowly and he put his coffee-cup down, a strange expression on his face. 'Actually, I'm starting to think they might be very much my thing, Dr O'Brien.'

The conversation had gone from light-hearted to deadly serious in the blink of an eye and her heart gave a little jump. 'What's that supposed to mean?'

'Just that I've been doing a lot of thinking over the past week.' He threw a wry smile in her direction. 'Given that there was no chance of getting any sleep, thanks to you, I spent my nights thinking. It was that or dig a large hole in the garden.'

'Why would you need a large hole in your garden?'

'I don't *need* a hole, but digging is the only way I know of getting rid of frustration. And believe me...' he folded his arms across his chest and looked her straight in the eye, '...at the moment I've got more frustration than I know how to deal with.'

She blushed. She could have told him that she felt exactly the same way, but she didn't want to admit that.

She was trying to move on. To put what they'd shared behind them. How could she do that if they kept raking it up every time they were together? They had to ignore the chemistry between them. They had to ignore the way they felt about each other.

'It's time I went.' She spread her hands in a nervous gesture and backed towards the door. 'I promised Archie a day on the beach and—'

'Wait! Dammit, don't just walk out on me again!' He ran a hand over his jaw and cursed under his breath. 'Last time we spoke about this I said all the wrong things to you. I know I was clumsy.'

'You weren't clumsy, Josh,' she said quietly, 'you were honest, and there's nothing wrong with being honest.'

'I was clumsy because what I wanted wasn't straight in my head.' His eyes burned into hers. 'But it's straight now.'

She stared at him. 'What do you mean?'

'I mean that I know exactly what I want now.' His voice was rough. 'It's all suddenly very clear.'

She couldn't breathe. *Couldn't move.* 'And what do you want, Josh?'

'You.' His eyes didn't shift from hers. 'I want you, Kat. All to myself. For ever.'

A thrill of excitement flashed through her but she stopped it dead, reminding herself that nothing had changed.

'We've been through this—'

'No.' He lifted a hand and shook his head. 'We haven't been through this. You've made certain assumptions about me, assumptions that I wasn't in a position to correct, but now I am.'

'Josh—'

'Let's look at the facts. You won't let yourself get involved with me because you think I'll hurt Archie,' he said quietly. 'But I'm not going to hurt him, Kat. I love him. In a different way to the way I love you, that's true, but I still love him.'

She stood frozen to the spot, frightened to disturb the dream by speaking.

'I can see you don't believe me.' His voice was hoarse and he stepped towards her and took her hands in his. 'But it's true. I love you and I love your son, and I would do anything in my power to prevent either of you from ever being hurt.'

Would she wake up? If she spoke, *would she wake up?*

He cupped her face in his hands and forced her to look at him. 'I didn't know anything about children until Archie came on the scene, and I still don't know much, but I'm learning, Kat. I swear to you, I'm learning as fast as I can. And do you know what?' He stared down into her face, the expression on his handsome face intensely serious. 'I understand now why you would sacrifice yourself to keep your son

happy because I have those feelings, too. I
don't know where they came from, but I have
those feelings, too.'

She swallowed. 'Josh—'

'Let me finish. You want to protect Archie
from me, but you don't need to do that, Kat. I
also want to protect him. I want to be a part
of his future.' He stroked her cheek gently with
his fingers. 'I want to share Archie with you.
I want to be there for him when he falls over
and...' He sucked in a breath and hesitated.
'And I want to be there for him the first time
a girl breaks his heart, the way you're breaking
mine now.'

She stared at him and tried to make her
voice work, breathlessly aware of the brush of
his fingers. '*I'm* breaking your heart? How?'
Her heart bumped against her chest. '*How* am
I breaking your heart, Josh?'

'By not trusting me. By not saying yes.'

She blinked. 'But—'

'Dammit, I've told you that I love you! And
that I love Archie!' He released her and spread
his hands in a gesture of exasperation. '*What
more do you want to hear?* I love everything

about you. I love the fact you're so independent. I love the fact that you don't care if your hair gets messed up by the wind. But most of all I love the fact that you love your child so much you'll run half-naked into a stranger's house to make sure he's safe. I love you and you're breaking my heart because you're not saying any of the things you're supposed to say!'

'What am I supposed to say, Josh?'

He stared at her in exasperation. 'You're supposed to say that you'll marry me. That's what you're supposed to say!'

There was a long silence. A silence that was suddenly bursting with promise.

'But you haven't asked me, Josh.' Suddenly she felt weak. 'You haven't asked me to marry you.'

His gaze dropped to her mouth and he frowned. 'I haven't?'

'No.' Her mouth curved into a smile that she couldn't hold back. 'You haven't. Maybe you forgot.'

He cleared his throat and dragged his eyes up to meet hers. 'Maybe I did.'

'So...' She gave a shrug. 'Are you going to do something about that?'

His mouth curved into a slow smile and he stepped towards her and dragged her into his arms.

'Wow.' Archie ran into the kitchen and skidded to a halt. '*Major* lip lock.'

Kat freed herself and gaped at her son. 'What did you say? *Where* did you hear that expression?'

Archie gave a shrug and scuffed his foot on the floor. 'Summer camp?'

Kat made a mental note to rethink summer camp for the following year. 'Josh and I were just...' She cleared her throat. 'We were just...'

'I know.' Archie's voice was patient. 'You were cuddling. That's all right. You don't have to explain. I know about that. Sometimes girls like being cuddled.'

'They do, indeed.' Josh shot a last, lingering look at Kat and strolled over to the boy. 'Hey, Arch.' He hunkered down so that they were on the same level. 'You remember this morning when you mentioned that sleepover? I'm thinking of taking you up on your invitation.'

'Cool!' Archie's face brightened and then fell. 'Trouble is...' he eyed Josh's shoulders doubtfully '...you're *definitely* too big for my snuggle sack.'

Josh ran a hand over his roughened jaw and gave a nod. 'I probably am. But I'm hoping your mum will find me somewhere else to sleep. This sleepover...' He cleared his throat. 'How would you feel if I did it quite often?'

'How often?'

'How would you feel about every night?'

'Wow.' Archie stared at Kat. 'Every night?'

Her heart jumped into her mouth as she looked at her son. 'How would you feel about that, Archie?' Her voice was soft. 'Josh wants to marry us.'

'*Us?*' Archie pulled a face. 'Yuck. Do I have to wear a dress and stuff like the girls in school? They're always trying to play weddings and it's just *gross.*'

Josh laughed. 'You don't have to wear a dress. And I'm not marrying *you* exactly, I'm marrying your mum. Or I'm hoping to. It's just that you come as a pair, so she wants to know that you're all right with the idea before she says yes.' His eyes rested on Kat for a moment. 'And I'm really hoping she's going to say yes.'

'You want to marry my mum?' Archie looked uncertain. 'But that would make you my dad.'

Josh took a deep breath. 'That's right.'

'Would you teach me to do knots? Mum's hopeless at knots.'

Kat gasped. 'Archie!'

He was still looking at Josh. 'Would you?'

Josh nodded, his face serious. 'I'd like that. And you could help me do up the boat.'

Archie thought hard and then nodded. 'Sounds cool.' He frowned. 'Would you make me eat broccoli?'

Josh rubbed a hand over the back of his neck and thought hard. 'Well...' He looked at Kat for inspiration. 'It's certainly important to eat vegetables...'

'I like carrots.'

'Well, that's fine, then.' Josh gave a shrug, man to man. 'So, what's the problem?'

A smile spread across Archie's face. 'No problem. You can marry us. Can't he, Mum?'

Kat swallowed back the lump in her throat. 'I suppose he can.' Her voice cracked. 'If he really wants to.'

Josh rose to his feet and scooped Archie into his arms. 'Oh, I really want to.' He leaned forward to kiss her gently, her son held securely in his arms. 'I really, *really* want to.'

MEDICAL ROMANCE™

Large Print

Titles for the next three months…

July

HER CELEBRITY SURGEON	Kate Hardy
COMING BACK FOR HIS BRIDE	Abigail Gordon
THE NURSE'S SECRET SON	Amy Andrews
THE SURGEON'S RESCUE MISSION	Dianne Drake

August

NEEDED: FULL-TIME FATHER	Carol Marinelli
THE SURGEON'S ENGAGEMENT WISH	Alison Roberts
SHEIKH SURGEON	Meredith Webber
THE EMERGENCY DOCTOR'S PROPOSAL	Joanna Neil
TELL ME YOU LOVE ME	Gill Sanderson
THE DOCTOR'S COURAGEOUS BRIDE	Dianne Drake

September

HIS SECRET LOVE-CHILD	Marion Lennox
HER HONOURABLE PLAYBOY	Kate Hardy
THE SURGEON'S PREGNANCY SURPRISE	
	Laura MacDonald
IN HIS LOVING CARE	Jennifer Taylor
HIGH-ALTITUDE DOCTOR	Sarah Morgan
A FRENCH DOCTOR AT ABBEYFIELDS	Abigail Gordon

MILLS & BOON®

Live the emotion

0606 LP 1P Medical